Reviews

An accurate portrayal of the CIA in action during the Cold War, and a story seldom told of the lives of case officers in the Clandestine Service.

—Peter S. Koromilas
A retired CIA Operations Officer

A riveting tale of service in the espionage trenches of the Cold War. A high-wire struggle. The pace is fast, the writing crisp, and the story authentic.

—Lee G. Mestres
A former CIA Operations Officer

Haunting characters enmeshed in a web of international significance create an intriguing first novel. Mr. Estes knows all the aspects of the spy game and how it reacts to success or failure.

—P. F. Marston
Author

THE MISSION

THE MISSION

CIA IN THE BALKANS

A Novel by

R. E. Estes

iUniverse, Inc.
New York Lincoln Shanghai

THE MISSION
CIA IN THE BALKANS

All Rights Reserved © 2003 by Ronald E. Estes

No part of this book may be reproduced or transmitted in any form or by any means, graphic, electronic, or mechanical, including photocopying, recording, taping, or by any information storage retrieval system, without the written permission of the publisher.

iUniverse, Inc.

For information address:
iUniverse, Inc.
2021 Pine Lake Road, Suite 100
Lincoln, NE 68512
www.iuniverse.com

ISBN: 0-595-28079-X (pbk)
ISBN: 0-595-65732-X (cloth)

Printed in the United States of America

To my wonderful family, who endured a great deal while I gained the experience necessary to write this book. And especially to my wife, Luba, whose good humor, patience, dedication to proofreading and editing, accompanied by great enthusiasm and encouragement, enabled me to finish it. Also, to Fran Schar, my neighbor and friend, whose kind and professional advice and experienced editing skills made this text readable.

*Dead spies
Are those for whom
We deliberately create
False information;
They then pass it on
To the enemy.*

—Sun-Tzu
The Art of War

Part I

Central Prison; Sofia, Bulgaria

Chapter 1

Kolev lay on his back on the bunk, his hands clasped behind his head, staring at the light bulb suspended from the ceiling of his cell. He had nothing else to look at. The pale green walls were bare and there was no window; the only sound came from the faucet's steady drip in the sink. In the narrow hallway outside his cell he heard the echoing sound of the guard's hobnailed boots on the concrete. The guard stopped, fumbled with the keys and opened the cell door.

"On your feet, Kolev, and face the wall!" he commanded.

Kolev stood and assumed the position he had taken so many times for so many years. The guard cuffed Kolev's hands behind him, led him down the hallway and pushed him into a small interrogation room. A tall man dressed in suit and tie sat behind the desk. He had large brown eyes, a high forehead, and curly black hair graying at the temples. A hint of a smile was on his lips. He motioned for Kolev to sit on a chair facing the desk.

"Free the prisoner's hands!" he ordered. He offered a cigarette and gazed steadily at the prisoner before speaking.

"Are you Ivan Kolev?" the man asked softly.

"Yes sir, prisoner number 99576."

"Kolev, my name is Markov. I'm from the State Prisoner Review Board. We've been appointed to review the status of all those imprisoned by the former Communist government. That is to say, those imprisoned who were not convicted of theft, robbery or violent crimes against their fellow citizens, and such other acts of common criminality. You, Mister Kolev, were convicted of espionage and sentenced to life in prison."

"Yes, sir, that's correct," Kolev replied, trying to guess the cost of Markov's double-breasted suit and silk necktie.

"I've read your file. However, we've discovered that files created by the former Communist government do not always reflect the real reasons behind criminal charges, or how evidence was gathered to substantiate those charges. Your new government recognizes that the former regime imprisoned many people for political reasons, and often created evidence to support criminal charges. I must make it quite clear to you: I'm not here to give you hope that you may be found innocent of charges made against you. The review we'll conduct is to ascertain the truth of the charges made against you, and if the sentence was just. We're not here to seek ways to arrange your release. Do you understand?"

Kolev took a long drag on his cigarette, and pursing his lips, blew a thin stream of smoke toward the ceiling.

"Yes, sir," he said. "Ascertain...?"

"Yes, ascertain, to determine, to find out. If we find that you were falsely charged, or not given reasonable legal representation at your trial, your file will be sent to the judicial system for review. And that could, I repeat *could*, lead to a change in your legal status. Do you understand?"

"Yes, sir," said Kolev, running a hand over close-cropped hair.

"Do you have any questions?"

"Mister Markov, sir, I have been a prisoner for eleven years and didn't commit espionage against Bulgaria. I tried to serve the Bulgarian government. No, sir, I have no questions, but I have a lot to say if you'll let me. No one has ever listened."

"Okay. My job is to listen to you. I want to know how this began. How'd you wind up here? Your file shows that you came from a simple background, and even had an uncle with a good position in the Communist Party. The file also says you escaped from Bulgaria. How was it that you became involved with the former internal security service? If you believe you were wrongfully imprisoned, tell me why. Take your time. Tell me the whole story, but stick with the facts, and be as precise as you can about dates, who did what—that sort of thing. I don't want to hear a bunch of whining, but I do want to know what transpired causing you to be here with a life sentence. I will interrupt you when you tell me things I don't care about. Have another cigarette."

He pushed the cigarette pack forward, leaned back, crossed his arms and waited.

Kolev looked like a man who had seen hard times. Life in prison had been difficult, the daily routine monotonous and the inmates dangerous. The prison held political prisoners, but many others came from all walks of life—common criminals and perverts. All considered him a traitor. Even those in prison for political crimes considered themselves loyal Bulgarians, but a prisoner convicted of espionage was an enemy.

He had been attacked many times. He had entered prison with broad shoulders, rippling muscles and the movements of an athlete. Gone was his cheerful demeanor, the quick smile that made his eyes sparkle. He had learned to show no emotion. His eyes were dull, cheeks hollow. The gray prison garb hung loosely—several sizes too large. An attack in the dining hall some years before broke off one of his front teeth. The prison dentist pulled what was left of the tooth, offering no replacement. His right eyelid drooped because another attack left scar tissue over the eye. He kept his head down to avoid looking others in the eye. Prisoners learned quickly that direct eye contact was often interpreted as a challenge.

Kolev suddenly realized the impact this interview might have on his future. Instinct told him to choose his words carefully. Somehow he must make this man Markov believe him.

"Thank you. Thank you very much for this chance," he said. "I don't know where to start—perhaps from the very beginning."

"That would seem appropriate. Please do."

Markov took a notepad and a pen from his coat pocket and placed them on the desk. Kolev fumbled with the pack, took out a cigarette and lighted it from the butt between his fingers. He propped an elbow on the desk and rested his forehead in his hand. Markov noticed that Kolev's hand trembled slightly. Kolev stared at the ceiling, shifted his weight and began.

He said he had been born on a collective farm near the town of Asenovgrad, south of Plovdiv. His father worked there as a carpenter and his mother worked in the kitchen, preparing mid-day meals for workers on the collective. The collective provided them a home with two rooms: his parents' bedroom, and a larger room where he slept. In that room his mother cooked their meals on a small wood burning stove, and they ate at a large table in the center of the room. The toilet was outside.

His father was tall and muscular with crew cut black hair and a large drooping mustache. He was an unhappy man, with eight years of education, and his life revolved around hard work and almost daily explanations of how he hated Turks, Macedonians and Greeks. The order of their importance changed with his mood. "Them damn people, they all the same," he always added. "And we got too damn many of them in this country." He became more loquacious about the subject, and louder, on Saturday nights after five or six stiff drinks of rakia. His mother, a short, plump woman, would giggle at her husband. For Kolev's mother life was a pleasant journey, and she laughed often and hugged Kolev at every opportunity.

To increase their meager income, workers at the collective cut wood in addition to growing crops. Kolev remembered his childhood as happy. He enjoyed being around farm animals, and school was fun because he could play with the other children.

"When I finished secondary school," he continued, "I served my time in the army, got in no trouble, as many did, and did a good job because the army wasn't bad. Work was harder on the collective, and in the army we always had plenty to eat and a warm place to sleep. After basic training I was stationed in a tank battalion near Ruse as a mechanic. I tried to stay in the army but my application was rejected even though I used my uncle in the Communist Party as a reference. After I got out, the Communist Party sent me back to the collective where I worked as a tractor mechanic."

Kolev didn't tell Markov why his uncle didn't endorse Kolev's attempt to stay in the army. It was his secret and would remain so until the day he died. It tormented him. When Kolev was thirteen years old, his uncle had visited the collective. Even then he was recognized as an influential member of the Communist Party. He had been quartered in a special house the collective reserved for important official visitors. The uncle requested that a certain teen age girl show him around the collective, and the young girl had been pleased to be so honored. Kolev, who had been collecting brush for a wood fire some distance from the collective's main buildings, saw his uncle and the girl enter an abandoned log cabin. Almost immediately the girl began screaming and crying. Kolev was transfixed by the horror and did nothing to help the girl. When the girl came running out of the cabin her lips were bloody, her blouse was torn and she had terror in her eyes. She went running toward her home sobbing. The uncle came out adjusting his clothes and saw Kolev standing a short distance away. Kolev ran home, and he told no one.

Perhaps somewhere deep in the reaches of Kolev's mind lay the prospect that once he fled from Bulgarian he could also flee that terrible memory.

Markov leaned forward, picked up the pen with both hands and rolled it between his fingers. Then he wrote on the pad, *"Doesn't make sense. How could intelligence service have interest in simple man, tractor mechanic—limited education and experience?"*

"Then I…"

Markov raised his hand to stop Kolev and asked, "Did you ever travel outside Bulgaria while you were in the army?"

Before Kolev could answer, a guard knocked on the door and entered. "Mister Markov," he said, "there's a telephone call for you. You may take it in the room at the end of the hall."

"Thank you," Markov said. He rose and left the room. The guard remained standing just inside the door, behind Kolev.

Kolev didn't turn to look at the guard, but instead hung his head, staring at his clasped hands. His mind raced. How much did Markov know about what happened in Greece?

Markov re-entered the room and returned to his seat. The guard left. Markov unbuttoned his coat, extended his arms and tugged his shirt cuffs below those of his suit coat.

He straightened his tie, picked up his pen and said, "I believe I asked you if you had traveled outside Bulgaria while you were in the army."

"Yes, sir, I did. Late in the first year of my service a joint training exercise was held with Soviet, Hungarian and Czech armies in eastern Czechoslovakia near the city of Kosice." He paused, and with a shrug said, "I've heard that Slovakia is now an independent country—hard to believe. But anyway, two battalions of infantry and my battalion were sent to take part. It was very interesting. Our tanks were transported by rail, and the infantry traveled with us in trucks.

"It took us three days to get there. We were so crowded you couldn't lie down to sleep and we ate nothing but cold, canned rations. The exercise lasted three days. A line of defense was formed east of Kosice to repel Czech invaders from the west. We saw a lot of Soviet troops, and *God*, did they look shabby. Parts of their uniforms didn't match. None of us looked much better, but at least our uniforms matched. The Soviets had good weapons, though." With a flick of his hand as if to dismiss the thought, he said, "Many of the Soviets we met were drunk, but the Czechs were sober, very well dressed and with newer equipment in better condition than we and the Soviets had.

"The exercise didn't go well for us; at least we didn't think so. The briefing at the end of the exercise showed that our forces stopped the enemy, who suffered great losses. But in our sector, and the Soviet sector to the north of us, the Czechs rolled right through us. In fact, they ended up behind us. I don't know how they judged such things, but we thought we lost.

"My group had a little party with about fifteen Soviet soldiers from an infantry company before we left for home. We supplied bread, cheese and fruit, and the Soviets supplied the vodka. Lots of it. They didn't have much food to offer. One played the accordion. They danced, and they could really dance—some wild gypsy looking dances, maybe Cossack or something. We enjoyed it. We sang some of our traditional songs, and they said we sang well. On the way home everybody agreed that we would rather be in the Bulgarian army than the Soviet."

Markov raised his hand to stop Kolev. He leaned back, clasped his hands behind his head, stared at the ceiling and sighed. After a moment he lowered his hands and asked, "Did you meet any other foreigners there besides Warsaw Pact soldiers?"

"No, sir."

"Hmm—go on."

Kolev didn't like it that Markov raised his hand to stop him. It was clear he didn't want to hear more about that subject, but Kolev didn't know what to say next.

Markov wasn't sure what to ask. He wanted as quickly as possible to get to that part of Kolev's background where he was allegedly recruited by a foreign intelligence service. Markov knew nothing about intelligence or internal security matters. He had been an administrative officer in the Ministry of Justice when he was assigned to work with the Prisoner Review Board. The former internal security service had destroyed all of its files when the Communist government fell, so all he had to work with was the transcript of Kolev's trial.

It was Markov's daughter's tenth birthday, and his brother; his wife and their children were coming for dinner. He had to stop on the way home to buy something for his daughter and buy a bottle of rakia to drink with his brother at dinner. Glancing at his watch, he realized the interview could continue for hours.

"Tell me how you escaped from Bulgaria," Markov said.

"Okay," Kolev said, "I'll explain that." He told Markov that after the army, life on the collective farm was boring. He didn't get along well with his father because his father expected him to marry some farm girl and spend the rest of his life on the collective. But he had seen Ruse, the Danube River and, in the army, had met people from different parts of Bulgaria who had done many interesting things. Opportunities existed for a young man. He didn't want to spend the rest of his life on the collective farm as a tractor mechanic.

"You work all day. Not much money. Get drunk on Saturday night. You must know what life was like on the collectives. We worked five and a half days a week. Nobody cared about what got done. If there were potatoes in the ground and a freeze was coming, nobody worked extra to get the potatoes in. When time came to quit on Saturday, everybody quit and the potatoes froze in the ground.

"My father and I argued a lot about it, and my mother cried every time we yelled at each other. My uncle, my father's brother, had a good job in the regional Communist Party, but I couldn't go to him for help. He made good money, but he didn't help us and we didn't see him often. He seemed to look down on my father and didn't appear to like me.

"My buddies from the collective and I could afford to go to Plovdiv about once a month. In Plovdiv there were cars, restaurants we couldn't afford to eat in, and stores with clothes we couldn't afford to buy. We saw lots of pretty girls who were well-dressed and who spoke well, not at all like the girls at the collective. But the girls in Plovdiv would have nothing to do with us.

"A year or so after I got out of the army I had a big fight with my boss. He was the general manager of the whole collective. He complained about my work, but hell, the tractors were old; we had no spare parts or anything. We didn't even have proper tools. He told my father, who gave me hell, and called me lazy and a disgrace to the family. But I got even with the boss."

"How?"

"I wrote a letter to the head of the Communist Party in Asenovgrad and mailed it from Plovdiv. Actually, I printed the letter so they couldn't recognize my handwriting. I wrote that the general manager was stealing produce from the collective and selling it on the black market, and printed the name of his deputy as the one who wrote the letter."

"Was he doing that?" Markov asked.

"I don't know—I just said that."

So, what happened?"

"Oh, boy, there was hell to pay! People from the Communist Party, along with a bunch of policemen, came to the collective. They stayed for days going over the books; you know—doing an audit, questioning people."

"What did they find?"

"Nothing. They quickly realized the deputy hadn't written the letter, and they didn't find anything wrong. They left, but it sure caused a lot of excitement at the collective."

"Well, you didn't accomplish anything, did you?"

"No, not really. But the boss sure was scared for a few days, and I enjoyed that. Anyway, not long after that I decided to leave. I wish now I hadn't. Life was awful there, but it was better than this."

Kolev helped himself to the cigarettes on the table. He lit one, inhaled deeply, and blew the smoke down into his lap. He kept his head down for a moment, and when he looked up Markov saw there were tears in his eyes. Kolev shook his head, cleared his throat and wiped his eyes with the sleeve of his shirt. Markov waited, quickly running his hands through his coat pockets, pretending he was looking for something and that he hadn't noticed.

"Tell me Kolev," Markov asked, "were you ever arrested during the time you worked at the collective?"

"Not really," he replied.

"What do you mean, not really?"

"Well, once when several of us from the collective were in Plovdiv we got a little drunk. As we were leaving a bar, I bumped a guy who was with four or five others trying to enter the bar. We had an argument and I hit him, knocking him down. It only takes six or eight beers to make me brave, but one of the guys with him hit me from behind, and I went down too. A fight broke out between the two groups. I'm not a good fighter, and proved it by getting knocked down two more times. The last time I decided not to get up. The police arrived and broke up the fight by swinging their clubs at anyone standing. One of the policemen yelled at me to get up, and then he kicked me in the back. It felt like my back was broken, and it hurt for weeks. Well anyway, they threw all of us into two vans and took us to the police station. There they took our names and where we were from and put us in cells. The next morning, those of us from the collective were told to return directly to the collective—just get out of Plovdiv. The other guys were from Plovdiv, and they probably let them go also, I don't know. We weren't charged with anything, so I don't count that as being arrested. Do you?"

Markov decided he must be more specific. Each question he asked had provoked more details than he had interest in. This was his first prisoner interview, and he wished he had more experience. This could be interminable.

"Kolev, I'm interested in how you escaped and when you were recruited by a foreign intelligence service."

"Yes, sir, I know, but you should know what made me escape. You see, I got in trouble over that fight. My uncle learned about it and called my father. My father and I had another big argument, and he threatened to kick me out of the house. I wanted to leave then, but didn't have the money, and it took me almost six months to save what I thought would be enough. No trips to Plovdiv—nothing.

"On our visits to Plovdiv we had gone to movies where they showed scenes of Sofia—such a great city. I decided to go there and find work, leave and never go back. The only thing I would miss would be my mother.

"I never did go back, but for reasons I never dreamed. My mother came to visit me three times here in prison. My father never did come. Now they're both dead."

"You may omit telling me about problems with your family. That will have no bearing on the review of your case. Go on."

"Yes, sir. Well, so when I'd saved some money, I packed a small bag with a few clothes—not very many things, but I did take a coat and tie to look nice when I went to ask for a job—then went to the kitchen to see my mother. For the first time, I told her my plans. She started to cry and hugged me. She gave me the few levas she had. Her hand was shaking. She said, 'Please let me know where you are.' I left and didn't say goodbye to my father. Oh! Sorry, you said that's not important. The afternoon bus to Plovdiv got me to the station in time to take the evening train to Sofia."

Kolev paused, hoping that Markov would indicate whether he was providing too much detail, but Markov was looking down at the note pad.

"In Sofia I went to a small inn, but I couldn't stay there long because it cost twelve levas a night, and I had less than a hundred. I tried for days to find a job, and went everywhere. The Communists always said there was no unemployment in Bulgaria. They may have been right. Somebody had taken every job I asked about, and I must have been the only unemployed person in Bulgaria. Eventually I learned that it was necessary to have a statement from my regional Communist Party, saying it was okay for me to work in Sofia.

"After three days I moved out of the inn to save money for food and started sleeping on a park bench. I had only enough money left to buy one good meal a day for about three more days, so I picked through hotel garbage barrels for extra food. You had to be careful doing that because in those days if the police caught you, you'd get arrested for vagrancy."

Kolev paused, ran a hand through his hair and scratched his head. He was hoping Markov would react to what Kolev was telling him. But Markov said nothing, so Kolev continued.

"I began to worry. I couldn't go back to the collective, so I thought about leaving Bulgaria and escaping to the West. You know, the West where everybody is rich, has a car, a big house, good clothes, and where you still don't have to work very hard. But I didn't know how to escape.

"Then I met a guy about my age at an outdoor café where I bought a cup of coffee for my lunch. We talked and walked around downtown Sofia for several hours. In fact, he bought me a beer. He was in Sofia to visit his aunt."

Markov placed his hands together, palms up as if begging. "I don't need that kind of detail," he said, "unless this person played some role in your case."

"He didn't really." Kolev paused, ran a hand over his chin, then continued. "Well, yes, he did, actually, but he didn't know it. He was from Melnik, at the south end of the Pirin Mountains, just north of the Greek border. He had been a border guard and had been posted near his home on the border. I didn't tell him I was planning to escape, but during the day he told me a lot about the border and the difficulties in trying to cross it illegally."

"What did he tell you?"

"Well, he said that where he was stationed each border guard post usually had one platoon, about thirty men, headed by a lieutenant, or sometimes a captain. The guards worked in three shifts, eight hours each, or in bad weather as little as two hours before being replaced. In some places they guarded more than three kilometers of the border. A barbed wire fence along the border wasn't well-maintained. In some places mines had been planted in a plowed strip on the north side of the fence, but most had been in the ground more than twenty years. He said that in many places where a steep slope met the fence there was no plowed strip and no mines. I asked about dogs, and he said each post had two or three. They were seldom used for patrolling, but more often were used for tracking if the guards suspected someone had crossed the border from Greece. Watchtowers had been built here and there, but at night or in bad weather guards didn't man them. He said guards were briefed that the Greeks sent agents across the border into Bulgaria as spies. His job was to catch them, and he was authorized to shoot them. Each night they placed an ambush on a path in one of the valleys. Those ambush places were changed almost every night, and his platoon manned only one a night."

Markov leaned forward, his eyes narrowing.

"Why did he tell you all of this?"

"He thought his military service was very exciting, and he wanted to impress me that he had serious responsibilities as a border guard. He did, too. He gave me many things to think about, and by the time we separated, I knew how I would escape to the West. Unfortunately, I would learn a great deal more about how to cross that border before the end of the next year."

"Fine, but tell me now how you did it the first time," Markov said.

Chapter 2

Markov pushed his chair back, rose and crossed the room, his hands clasped behind his back. "Go on, Kolev," he said, "I just want to stretch a bit."

Kolev, his head down, was watching Markov out of the corner of his eye. He said that during the next two days he had prepared for his escape. He found a backpack in the trash behind a youth hostel. It had a broken strap, but could be carried on one shoulder. He grabbed a cheap, plastic canteen from a bicycle parked outside a bookstore, and with all but a few of his remaining levas he bought bread and cans of beans. From outdoor stands he stole an orange here, an apple there. In that way, he said, he gathered enough food to last a few days if he ate sparingly.

"On the day I chose to leave—"

"Just a minute," Markov said, "before you continue, did you meet with any foreigners during your stay in Sofia? I want to know when you first made contact with the foreign intelligence service. Did you visit any foreign embassies?"

"No, sir. I met them in Greece. The only real conversation I had in Sofia was with the former border guard. I would've been afraid to go to a foreign embassy."

Markov returned to his chair and wrote on the pad. "Go on."

Kolev said that the day he left he took a bus to the western suburbs of Sofia and walked to the highway to Blagoevgrad. He caught a ride in a truck to Stanke Dimitrov, and from there another truck took him to Blagoevgrad. He told both drivers he was going to Melnik, where he had been offered a job as an automobile mechanic. Farther south another truck dropped him outside a small village, and although it was only mid-afternoon, he spent the rest of the day and that night in trees several hundred meters off the highway. The next day he arranged a ride in a truck delivering beer to Kulata, the border crossing point into Greece.

"I got out of the truck north of Kulata because the former border guard told me about a checkpoint there. From the highway I walked east, starting to climb into the hills, then waded across a shallow river, and stayed south of the road to Petrovo, still climbing. No one was around except to the north where I saw a shepherd with a flock of sheep. He was over a kilometer away, and didn't appear to see me. I walked until dark, and then ate and drank a lot from my canteen, because of a small stream nearby where I could fill it again.

"I tried to sleep among some trees, but it was cold, and without a warm jacket it was difficult. But I must've slept several hours, because when I awoke the sun was up, and not fifty meters from me a young boy was herding a flock of sheep. The boy saw me and walked over—he must've been about twelve. He was a nice boy; he shared some bread with me and told me he was from a small village to the north. His village was collectivized with four other villages, and his father worked there as a farmer and his mother made cheese from goat milk. The collective sold the things they produced to a truck driver who picked the stuff up every day or so. The boy also asked me what I was doing there."

Markov turned sideways in his chair, propped an elbow on the desk and rested his forehead in his hand. Without looking up he asked, "Kolev, did this boy play some role in your escape? Is that why you're telling me this?"

"No, sir," Kolev replied. "Not directly, but it worried me that I'd let that boy get so close without seeing or hearing him. Nearer to the border it would have been stupid for me to let that happen again."

"What'd you tell him?" Markov asked, raising his head only slightly.

"I told him I was from Sofia and in training for the Bulgarian national ski team, visiting relatives near Kulata for a few days and hiking in the hills to toughen my legs. And I said I got lost the evening before and when it got dark decided to sleep there. He gave me directions back to Kulata and we parted.

"So he wouldn't suspect me, I started back toward Kulata, following his directions. But when I had passed out of sight I turned south for about half an hour and then turned east again."

Markov asked Kolev how he knew where he was going. "Did you have a compass?" Kolev said he didn't need a compass. He knew the direction of south because of where the sun rose. He planned to walk almost directly east from Kulata to where the mountains became higher and steeper, and at some point turn south again. Because of what the former border guard told him, he knew he had to do two things: reach the border at a place where the steep slope of a mountain lessened the chance of a plowed strip with mines in front of the fence; and, to avoid valleys where border guards could ambush him.

He said he walked all that day and saw no one. By afternoon he had entered steep mountains, and was tired by dusk. The area was heavily forested, with mold growing on stones and the base of some trees, and a musty smell of pine filled the air. He then stopped to eat and found that he had food only for another day or so. That night he slept among large boulders, and although he was cold again, he rested better because the boulders seemed to retain heat from the sun.

"I had a dream. I was running, and men were chasing me. My legs wouldn't move fast enough and the men were gaining on me. Before they caught me I woke up. The dream made me nervous and stayed on my mind all the next day.

"It was still dark when I awoke. I decided to start walking again because the sky was clear and the stars so bright it was easy to see. You see, it was safer for me to walk at night when nobody was around, because if I'd met someone in that area, unlike dealing with that shepherd boy, it would've been more difficult to explain why I was there. I started to walk southeast."

Markov chewed on his thumbnail, looking down.

"Am I telling you too much detail?" Kolev asked. "I want you to understand, because you have no idea how important this is to me. You told me not to expect to get out of here because of your review, but I'm innocent, and this is the first time in eleven years that anyone has given me a chance to talk about it."

Markov offered Kolev another cigarette. "I'm interested in the details of your escape. You said you met the foreign intelligence service in Greece," he said, "but I want to know if anyone helped you cross the border—if anyone made it easier for you."

"No one helped me," Kolev said. "I crossed by myself, and I'll tell you how, because it wasn't that difficult."

Markov rose, removed his coat and hung it on his chair. He loosened his tie, and said, "Go on, please continue."

"I had walked until about two hours after dawn and suddenly heard a vehicle approaching. About three hundred meters south a military jeep passed on a dirt road I hadn't seen. The jeep contained five soldiers, and all but the driver carried weapons. I was sure they were border guards and the border was close. We had been taught in the Army that citizens were not allowed in a border area without a pass, so I was scared. About an hour later, the jeep passed again, in the opposite direction, empty except for the driver. I hid there all day, and I worried about where he dropped those soldiers."

Kolev paused, trying to recollect the following night. The stars had been bright, he said, and he walked almost all night, climbing steadily. When the sun rose he was on the south slope of a steep mountain, and he saw a fence below, about two hundred meters away. But directly in front of it he noticed the plowed mine strip. He crawled into bushes and slept intermittently all day.

When the sun's last rays highlighted the ridges and ignored the valleys, he saw a steep ridge to the east, about a kilometer away that crossed the fence. About a hundred meters before the fence, trees on the slope had been cleared, and a dirt path, good enough for a jeep or truck, paralleled the barrier. He could see no plowed strip.

"It looked like a good place to cross, but it worried me that a deep valley separated the ridge I was on from the one to the east. The border guard had said the guards set ambushes in valleys at night. What if the jeep that passed me had dropped those soldiers in the valley for the night's ambush? It also concerned me that although I had plenty of water, my food was gone, and I was hungry. I needed to keep going."

At dusk, Kolev had begun to descend toward the valley, moving a few steps at a time, then pausing to listen. The only sound came from leaves, ruffled by a breeze. He moved in that manner for several hours. Nearing the valley floor he stopped to listen, and lay still for a long time.

"If an ambush had been prepared in the valley there should have been some noise. Soldiers couldn't remain in one position all night without talking. I heard nothing.

"I started again, but after no more than a hundred meters I heard a loud crashing among the trees. Several figures jumped up and ran in different directions. I panicked, yelled, turned and ran up the incline—right into a tree. I went down; but jumped up again and ran until I couldn't any more, expecting to be shot in the back at any moment.

"I lay on the ground, trying to catch my breath. My head ached. I had hit that tree with my forehead, and could feel warmth on my face. It felt like blood—you know, wet and sticky. When I wiped my face and hand with my handkerchief I found blood. But I heard nothing. No one was chasing me. No soldiers were calling or moving toward me.

"Suddenly, off to my left something moved. It was the silhouette of a large buck deer, with two or three does moving behind it. Damn! How stupid I felt, almost killing myself running from deer. But had there been an ambush in that valley, the soldiers would surely have heard me yell, the sound of running, and they would have come to investigate. You know, Mister. Markov, I was relieved. Obviously, no one had prepared an ambush."

Kolev noticed that Markov's eyes were riveted on his. Kolev took another cigarette, lighted it and inhaled deeply. He rested an elbow on the table, held his forehead, then ran a hand over his face. "You don't realize how glad I was, Mister. Markov. I was pretty damned scared."

"I can imagine," Markov said. "I would've been too. What'd you do next?"

Kolev said he started walking down into the valley again, but this time with less caution. After crossing the valley he began an arduous climb. It was tough going, he said, and the steep incline had forced him to stop every few minutes to rest. Just before dawn he reached the crest and turned south, down the steep slope toward the fence. About twenty meters inside the tree line he sat behind thick brush. Not long after, the first light began to penetrate the brush, shadows shortened and light bathed the ground before him. He could see the cleared area before the fence and the vehicle path, but no plowed strip. He waited.

"I don't know if it was nerves or hunger, but my stomach churned. I still had water in my canteen, but my knapsack was empty, so I left it, covering it with dirt and leaves.

"My right hand showed dried blood where I'd touched my face during the night, and I noticed blood on my shirt. My headache was better, but the lump over my left eye hurt to touch."

He said that toward the middle of the day he had heard a vehicle approaching from the west. It was a military jeep with a driver and one man with a rifle. It moved slowly, both men studying the ground on either side of the vehicle. It continued to the east and about an hour later it returned, this time at normal speed, then disappeared to the west. Kolev didn't see or hear anything else the rest of the day.

"Do you think they were looking for you?" Markov asked.

"No, I don't think so," Kolev said. "I think they were looking for footprints or signs that someone had passed, and they didn't seem very serious about it, because when they came back they were talking and laughing."

Markov clasped his hands and studied them a moment. He gnawed his upper lip and asked, "Could you see anything on the Greek side? Any Greek border guards?"

"No, sir," Kolev said. "I didn't see anybody, and I could see quite a ways into Greece. The slope to the fence leveled off on the Greek side, then the ground ran down into a cut—what do you call it?"

"A ravine?" Markov asked.

"Yeah, a ravine, and on both sides of that cut I could see wooded, high ridges. After I crossed the border I was going to head for that cut—that ravine.

"In late afternoon it started to rain. Thick clouds rolled in from the west, and they hung low over the area. God must have been watching over me, because that was a blessing."

"A blessing from God, huh? Are you a Christian?" Markov asked.

"No, not really. My mother believed and prayed sometimes, but my father didn't, and he ignored it. I was never baptized, and in fact have never been to church. It was discouraged, you know. It's just and expression, and sure as hell no one gives a prisoner a chance to be a Christian, at least not in this prison. I never thought about it. Would it help me if I were a Christian? I could become one, you know."

"No, no, forget it. Go on. I was just curious."

Kolev resumed his story. He said it had begun to rain hard, but with the storm and dark clouds he was able to stand and move around without fear of being seen.

"It felt good to get up and move my arms, but I was drenched and very cold. The wind picked up, making me colder.

"I couldn't really tell when dusk came, because it had grown so dark from the clouds and the rain that there was no sunset. The darker it became, the closer I moved to the cleared area in front of the fence, and when it had been almost totally dark for what seemed a couple of hours, I decided to go.

"I planned to cross that cleared area on my stomach, but it was raining so hard, and it was so dark, no one could have seen me from twenty meters away. So I sprinted to the fence and almost ran into the damned thing before I saw it. The fence was barbed wire. On my knees, I tried to raise the bottom strand, cutting both hands in the process. If it had been a few centimeters higher I could've made it.

"It was raining so hard, it was tough to do anything. The water kept running in my eyes. The higher strands were too close together to get between them, but in the ground, under the bottom strand, I discovered two flat stones, almost side by side. I began to dig out the first, taking so long I began to panic. I dug frantically, scooping dirt from around the stone, and finally it loosened. I removed it and started on the second, which was larger than the first, and that took what seemed forever. Despite the rain and the cold, I was sweating. My hands were raw and really hurt.

"Suddenly, a dog barked. I froze, my heart beating so fast I could feel it. I stood to run back to the tree line, then the dog barked again—twice more. It seems like yesterday. But the sound was from the Greek side of the border, and from far off. I sat and waited a few moments, and then started digging again. Within minutes I was able to move the stone—to rock it back and forth—and pull it out."

With the stones out of the ground, Kolev said, he squeezed his head and shoulders under the wire, but it caught the back of his shirt. He pulled with his hands and pushed with his legs and the shirt tore. He broke free, scrambled under the fence, rose to his feet and began running down the slope, but stumbled, fell and rolled several times. He ran a short distance farther, but stumbled and fell again. Finally, on his knees, the rain beating on his face, he began to cry. His arms raised to the sky, he shouted:

"I made it, by God, I made it!"

A dog barked, he said, but this time it sounded like a welcome.

Chapter 3

▼

Kolev placed both hands on the desk, straightened his arms and tilted his chair back. He grinned at Markov, exaggerating the gap in his front teeth. Markov smiled, unsure why Kolev was grinning, but willing to share the moment. "Yes, sir, Mister Markov, I did it, and I did it all by myself," Kolev said. He pumped his left fist in the air, allowing the chair to settle forward with a bang.

"After a while," Kolev continued, "I walked toward that cut, and within ten minutes started into it. I encountered trees, but mostly lots of low bushes, and in the dark I stumbled over them often. It would have been easier to wait until dawn, but I wanted to get as far away from the border as possible before first light.

"Suddenly a voice in front of me shouted, 'Halt!' All around me bolts of weapons slammed shut. I couldn't see anything, but heard voices yelling in Greek. I shouted, 'Don't shoot, I surrender!'"

Kolev said he remembered someone approaching, stepping in front of him and saying something in Greek. Kolev answered, "I'm Bulgarian, and I've escaped." The man directed a flashlight at Kolev's face and body while walking slowly around him. More soldiers appeared—maybe eight or ten, he said—with weapons and helmets, and ponchos over their uniforms. The soldier with the flashlight had motioned for Kolev to raise his hands, and when he did so another soldier approached from behind and searched Kolev carefully. When he finished, the soldier lowered Kolev's arms.

"I had walked into a Greek ambush, and I'll tell you, Mister Markov, sir, I was damned glad.

"They talked among themselves for a few minutes, and then formed a file, putting me in the middle, four or five soldiers ahead of me and some behind. They led me deeper into the, uh, ravine, and one of the men seemed to talk into a radio—it was too dark to see which one—and after about twenty minutes we came to a clearing where we met four more soldiers and two mules. We all stood still, the Greeks talking and shining flashlights on me.

"One soldier offered me a cigarette, and they held a poncho so I could light it. From one of the mules a soldier took a blanket out of a pack and put it around my shoulders. It felt good because it was still raining, and I was cold—and very tired."

"Did they give you any indication that they were expecting you?" Markov asked.

"No! They couldn't have been expecting me, because they didn't know I was coming. How could they?" Kolev, his voice rising, put both hands on top of his head and ran them over his cheeks. "And later, the interrogator mentioned something about the night I walked into their ambush."

"Okay, okay, what happened?"

"Well, both mules were loaded with packs, probably food and other supplies for the soldiers and food for the mules. They rearranged the packs, and when ready to leave they put me on a mule. One soldier led it while we moved on for a couple of hours. Just before dawn the rain stopped and the sky began to clear. I dozed off and almost fell off twice. I had never ridden a mule before, and never will again. It was better than walking, as tired as I was, but it was very uncomfortable.

"At first light we reached a building where many more soldiers were hanging around. Two led me inside to a large room, and I could see doors off that to several other rooms. One was a kitchen, I know, because they later brought me food from there, and they had a dining room too. I don't know where the soldiers slept, because the building wasn't big enough for that, and I didn't see any other buildings close by."

In the large room, he recalled, an officer sat behind a desk and eight or ten chairs lined the walls. A soldier led Kolev to stand in front of the desk, but the officer didn't look up or acknowledge Kolev's presence. A number of soldiers were standing around, and Kolev recognized some who had brought him there. The room smelled of cigarette smoke and the wet wool of uniforms. The officer finally asked the soldiers several questions, and each one snapped to attention when addressed.

"Suddenly, some soldiers started yelling to the soldiers outside. They called, 'Ioannaki! Ioannaki!' and in a minute or so a young soldier came running in. The officer spoke to him briefly, and the soldier turned to me, and in Bulgarian, said, 'Take everything out of your pockets and put it on the desk.' When I did that, he told me to sit down."

Kolev folded his arms and rocked several times. He looked at the ceiling as if to recall what happened next.

"The officer, maybe a lieutenant, began asking me questions, with the soldier interpreting. He asked my name and where I was from, and when I answered, another soldier pulled a chair to the end of the desk, sat and began making notes. The officer asked why I escaped, so I told him about life on the collective farm, about trying to find work in Sofia, and after no luck, deciding to try to get to the West."

What Kolev didn't know, was that that the Greek officer, a first lieutenant of infantry, who bore a long scar down the left side of his face—something he had picked up fighting Turks in Cyprus some ten years earlier—didn't like Bulgarians. He was approaching the end of his tour of duty at the border post, and bored with questioning refugees. They were all the same, uneducated peasants who knew nothing militarily significant. He had developed sympathy for his ancient forebear, Heraclitus, who had great disdain for the mediocrity of his fellow Ephesians. He wanted to return to a line unit, to command troops and win a promotion.

His voice a monotone, the lieutenant had told Kolev, "Explain how you escaped." Kolev had told him about his meeting with the former border guard in Sofia and what he had learned. The officer asked what he had seen in the border area and asked him to describe the border guard jeep he had seen with the armed men, and the weapons they were carrying. Kolev couldn't and explained that they were too far away. The officer asked how Kolev received the bruise on his forehead, and when Kolev told him, the officer shrugged and lit another cigarette.

"Kolev," Markov interrupted, rubbing his chin and surveying the ceiling, "until that point the Greeks had treated you well. Was that officer hostile?"

"No, no, he wasn't hostile; he simply ignored me. He seldom looked directly at me. When asking questions and listening to my answers he looked at the interpreter, not me. He seemed bored, and he smoked one cigarette after another as if he were more interested in smoking than talking to me. But anyway, I was starting to get warm, with the blanket around my shoulders, and was still really hungry.

"After many questions, I asked the interpreter if I might have a glass of water. He spoke to the officer. He kept asking me questions, but after a few minutes a soldier brought a small tray with a cup of coffee and a glass of water. My hands shook when I drank the coffee, and the officer noticed it. For the first time, he looked directly at me and asked if I was scared. I told him I was not, but that I was hungry and tired. He promised that after more questions I would be fed, and then I could sleep."

The officer had asked many questions about Kolev's military service: where he was trained, what units he served in and on what type of tanks he worked. He exhibited more than passing interest in the training exercise Kolev's battalion held in Czechoslovakia.

"Later, thinking back on that interrogation, I think the officer was only trying to learn what types of things I knew something about, because he didn't ask me details about anything. I don't think he cared what I told him."

After an hour or so of questioning, Kolev said, a soldier had taken him to a bathroom and given him soap and a towel and told him to bathe at one of the four showers. The water was cold, and when he finished he had to dress in the same wet clothes. Then he was taken to a small room with whitewashed, bare walls, a cot, a blanket, a small table, one chair and one small window, high on the wall. A crack spread several meters down one wall and a brown stain high on another indicated that the roof leaked. The interpreter said food would arrive shortly, and if Kolev needed something he should knock on the door.

Not long after, a soldier entered with a tray that he put on the table. He smiled at Kolev and left. The tray held a glass of cold water, a bowl of beans, with olive oil floating on the top, and a big chunk of bread in another dish, with half a raw onion, half a lemon and a few olives. Kolev ate ravenously, then lay on the cot and went immediately to sleep, wet clothes and all.

"In the morning, I was still asleep when the interpreter entered, shook me awake and told me to prepare to be moved. Another soldier brought a cup of coffee and a half loaf of bread. My clothes were almost dry by then, so I broke the bread in half and stuffed it in my pockets.

"After about a half an hour, they led me outside to a small army truck with canvas over the back. I recognized some of the soldiers who were standing around. We all smiled, and I said, 'Good morning,' in Bulgarian. They said, '*Kali emera*,' which I later learned means, 'good morning' in Greek."

Kolev paused, ran a hand across his mouth and rubbed his eyes. He was tired of talking; yet he had so much more to say.

"They put me into the back of the truck, and I sat on a bench along the side. Two soldiers sat down, one opposite me and one beside me. We then drove for several hours. The soldiers were friendly, but we couldn't talk, because they didn't speak Bulgarian, but they offered me cigarettes many times, and I shared my bread with them. When we passed pretty girls on the road they would yell and whistle, so I joined in, and we had a good time and laughed a lot. But those benches got awfully hard after a while, and the canvas top was so low we couldn't stand up fully."

His first view of the Aegean was unforgettable, he said. They had entered a large town, built on hillsides overlooking the sea. The water was a shimmering, deep blue, and the houses sparkled white in the bright sunshine. He later learned that the town was Kavalla. He couldn't see much from the back of the truck, which continued through the town on narrow cobblestone streets and turned south on a road paralleling the sea. The surface soon turned from asphalt to dirt, and after a few kilometers the truck turned off and passed through a gate guarded by two soldiers. Without stopping it entered a compound with a dirt surface that ended in front of a one-story building, a Greek flag over the entrance.

"The three of us, stiff and sore from riding on that uncomfortable bench, got out of the truck. Several soldiers emerged from the building, looked me over, and spoke with the soldiers who had come with me. They led me inside to a small room and motioned to a chair in front of a desk. Nothing happened for a few minutes, and the soldiers talked. I saw a large black box on the desk. I had no idea what it was.

"Then the door opened, and a tall, slender man entered, wearing civilian clothes. The soldiers stood at attention, and when the man spoke they left.

"The man shook hands and in excellent Bulgarian said, 'Welcome to Greece. Please stay seated and make yourself comfortable.' He sat at the desk, dropped a pack of cigarettes and matches on it, told me to help myself and pushed a button on the black box.

"I am an official of the Greek government," he said, and added that he was an interrogator. He told Kolev that they would work together often during the coming days. He said Kolev would be kept in a cell, not as a prisoner, but because there was no other place to house him. While there, he explained, Kolev would be provided three meals a day and allowed to use the bathroom whenever he wished, within reason. "Just call the guard stationed in the hallway outside your cell," he said. The interrogator said he would talk with Kolev a couple of hours each morning and each afternoon or evening, and ask him questions about Bulgaria and about himself.

"You'll answer them to the best of your ability," he said, "and when we finish with the questions—and we are convinced you have answered them truthfully—you'll be released and sent to a refugee camp in southern Greece. There the

World Council of Churches will begin the process of trying to resettle you in some Western country. If you aren't truthful, I'll know, and then we'll work together to determine why."

The interrogator had explained that many Bulgarian refugees passed through the interrogation center every year, and a certain percentage was discovered to have been dispatched to Greece as agents of the Bulgarian Intelligence Service. They had been trained, he added, to repeat a cover story designed to mask their whereabouts during their espionage training, and how they were assisted to cross the border. Those agents, he said, had been sent by the Bulgarian service to be processed through refugee channels for resettlement in the West without raising suspicion. Once in the West, the intelligence service would contact them and instruct them to begin conducting espionage or sabotage operations. His job, he said, was to screen every refugee to ensure that he was not on a mission for the Bulgarian service. If a refugee arrived in Greece, the interrogator said, pointing his finger at Kolev, and immediately admitted that he had been sent by the Bulgarian service, he would not be penalized, and if he provided details of Bulgarian instructions, he would be processed like every other refugee.

"If, however, he denies that he's on a mission for the Bulgarian service," he said, "and we later discover that in fact he is, and has tried to deceive us, he will be directed to a Greek military court martial. The penalty for working for a hostile foreign intelligence service on Greek soil is death by hanging. Do you fully understand everything I just told you? Do you have any questions?'

"No, sir," I told him, "I fully understand. I have no questions."

Kolev said the Greek paused, looking directly into his eyes. The interrogator didn't blink. The man's eyes matched the coal black fabric of his suit. He propped both elbows on the desk and put the tips of the long slender fingers of both hands together.

"'Good!' he said. 'Now I have one question for you. Think about your answer carefully. Are *you*, Ivan Kolev, on a mission for the Bulgarian Intelligence Service?'

"I didn't hesitate a moment, Mister Markov, and said loudly, 'No, sir, I'm not. I'm not a spy. I want to go to the West to find a decent job. Just that, and nothing more. I haven't been sent here by anyone.'

"He stared directly at me for a few seconds, and his stare made me nervous. 'Good, young man,' he said. 'If that's the truth, we'll get along fine, and you'll have a bright future.'

"With that, he stood, again pushed a button on the black box, shook hands with me and left. Almost immediately a soldier entered and motioned for me to follow him."

Markov looked at his watch, took a cigarette from the pack, lit it and blew the smoke toward the ceiling. "Did that man give you his name?" he asked.

"No, Mister Markov, and during all the time we spent talking—every day for a couple of weeks—he never used a name. But he knew a great deal about Bulgaria, more than I did."

"You said he spoke Bulgarian. Was he a Bulgarian?"

"No. He spoke Bulgarian fluently, but he had an accent. I don't think it was his native language."

The interrogator was Mitsos Panagoulis. His parents were Macedonian Greeks, and they both spoke Bulgarian. But they spoke Greek at home, and Mitsos heard Bulgarian only when his grandmother came to visit and at family reunions. Mitsos was fifty years old, and he had been an interrogator for the Greek Intelligence Service, KYP, for twenty-eight years. Tall and slender, he always wore a black suit, white shirt and tie when working. He had a habit of running his right thumb over the tips of the fingers of his right hand when conducting an interrogation.

In October, 1944, during the Bulgarian occupation of northern Greece, the Bulgarians retaliated against a Greek partisan ambush of a Bulgarian army unit by shooting every male over the age of fifteen in the town of Drama. Mitsos' father had been one of eighty-four men shot that day, and Mitsos, who was nine, and his mother had witnessed the shooting. Over the next several days Mitsos' mother became insane and he never saw her again. An aunt and uncle raised him. When he was drafted into the Greek army, because of his Macedonian background, he was sent to school to study Bulgarian, and after his discharge, he was hired by KYP. Mitsos had interrogated well over two thousand Bulgarian refugees, and he knew more about Bulgaria than anyone in the Greek government. His personnel record showed that during interrogations of refugees suspected of being agents of the Bulgarian Intelligence Service, he often had to be restrained from using "excessive physical violence" as an interrogation technique.

"He may have been a Greek Macedonian," Markov said. "I understand many of them speak Bulgarian, or at least their version of Bulgarian. In any case, continue."

"Well, the soldier took me to cell number seven. On the cot were underwear, khaki trousers, a khaki shirt and a pair of sandals, and the soldier motioned for me to change clothes. The cell was very much like the room they had put me in at the border post: bare white walls, one window, but this one had bars on it, and there was a small desk and one chair. For this room, however, the guard opened and closed the door with a key. I was locked in.

"Not long after I'd changed, a soldier brought me food, just greens, bread and a glass of water. I hadn't eaten anything but a piece of bread all day, and I was still hungry when I finished the food. Later they brought me soap, a razor and a towel.

"Nothing happened the next day. In the morning they brought cheese, olives and bread, and for the other meals the same kind of food they had given me at the border post. The food was monotonous, but it was tasty and enough."

"You don't have to tell me what they fed you," Markov interrupted.

"Okay, the food wasn't worth talking about anyway. They let me out of the cell in the afternoon to walk around a walled courtyard behind the building. The wall was high, much taller than I am, with a barbed wire roll on top of it. Others were being held in the center, because I could hear cell doors opening and closing, but I never saw anyone else in the courtyard except a guard by the door. After an hour or so they'd return me to the cell. That was the routine every day I was there, except for the morning and afternoon interrogation sessions with the Greek civilian."

"Fine," Markov said. "Now tell me what the interrogations were like."

For each session, Kolev said, a guard took him to one of many interrogation rooms, all of them the same, no windows and nothing on the walls, the usual bare light bulb hanging from the ceiling. The desk always held a bottle of water with two glasses, and Kolev could drink whenever he wanted. Black boxes in all interrogation rooms were recording machines. Every word was recorded.

Before the Greek interrogator began questioning Kolev, he reviewed the report of Kolev's initial debriefing at the border post and noted that the lieutenant who had questioned Kolev there had addressed his report to KYP headquarters in Kavalla. At the end he appended:

"**ATTENTION. OPERATIONAL NOTE:** This refugee, Kolev, has only a secondary education, but is more intelligent and articulate than the typical refugee we see at this post. He may be of some operational value."

The interrogator began with questions about Kolev's family, and asked his mother's full name, where and when she was born, her parents' names, and where and when they were born. He asked for the same information about her brothers and sisters, the names of the people they married, and the names of their children. He jotted on a pad what hours Kolev's mother worked, what she was paid, and what kinds of food she prepared at the kitchen where she worked.

Then he wanted the same information about Kolev's father and his relatives. The interrogator repeated some of those questions every few days, going from one to another rapidly to note whether he received the same answers each time.

He zeroed in on Kolev's uncle, who worked for the Communist Party, and asked many questions about him: where he worked, what his job was, when he joined the party and what rank he held. Kolev realized that he didn't know much about his uncle, and he couldn't answer the questions about where the uncle lived—except the town—and how much money he earned.

The interrogator asked what the collective produced, and what Kolev knew about officials at the collective. When Kolev answered questions about quotas the collective had to fill, how often Communist Party officials visited the collective and who they were, the interrogator made notes. He questioned Kolev about thefts on the collective and crimes in the region. Questions about military bases in the area lasted almost two days. After every session Kolev returned to his cell with his head spinning.

Then the interrogator turned to Kolev's background: where he went to school, what grades he made, the names of teachers, and what he knew about their personal lives. He had delved at length into Kolev's military service; where he was inducted, his basic training, the trainers, jotting down the dates when Kolev left training and was assigned to the tank unit at Ruse. He asked Kolev to describe in great detail the tanks he worked on, how often they broke down, the most common cause of breakdown, and the type and manufacture of the tools his unit used. He questioned Kolev about Soviet advisers assigned to his unit and what roles they played in the command structure. The interrogator focused on the frequency and objective of training exercises in which Kolev participated or had heard about. He took copious notes of Kolev's answers to questions about each of his officers, including how competent they were, how dedicated, and whether the troops they commanded respected them. The interrogator asked what kind of food Kolev's unit was served, both in garrison and in the field, how the food was prepared and how it was delivered. He wanted the names of any soldiers or officers who did not like military service, and of those who appeared to be anti-Communist, or were active and outspoken supporters of the Communist Party.

"I laughed when he asked the names of those who didn't like military service," Kolev said. "I told him we had eight hundred men in the battalion and I didn't know all their names. The interrogator laughed too, and said, 'It is the same in our army.'"

"I'm surprised the man had time to laugh," Markov interrupted. "Is this what interrogators do?" he added. "Do they ask so many questions about so many things? Who cares about such details?"

Kolev shrugged, pushed his chair back and stood. He put his hands on his hips, bent forward and backward from the waist and sat again.

"I don't know—his bosses probably," he said. "But I got tired answering them, and haven't told you about a lot of them yet. He asked lots of questions about the training exercise we had in Czechoslovakia, which units participated from each country and the number and types of tanks and personnel carriers each army used in the exercise. He asked about small arms the soldiers carried and what food they were given. I couldn't answer most of those questions, and explained that I had been a private and knew very little about the exercise, except what I could see around me. I told him my job during the exercise was repairing tanks because many broke down and needed repairs every day. Then he wanted to know how many tanks we took with us, and how many of them broke down, but I didn't know that, because our sergeant kept a log of how many we repaired and which ones. To me the tanks all looked the same. He wanted to know what repairs were most frequently required, and again I said that only our sergeant kept such records, but that I personally worked more on treads and clutches than anything else.

"He spent a couple of days questioning me about my escape, starting with the bus I took from Asenovgrad to Plovdiv. He wanted to know how much money I started out with, and before we finished, I had to account for almost every leva of it. When we discussed what time the train left Plovdiv for Sofia, he read from a book that looked like a train schedule. While he was reading it he asked me what time the train arrived in Sofia, and when I told him he put the book away.

"He questioned me about the inn where I stayed for a few days in Sofia, and looked that up in another book. When he finished, he nodded and put the book away. Then he asked me to name the hotels where I took food from the garbage barrels, and to name the hostel where I found the knapsack, but I didn't know the names. He wanted to know what happened to the knapsack, and said, 'You didn't have it when our patrol found you.' While I was explaining to him where I left it, he tapped a finger on the table, staring at me. 'Fine' he said, 'I accept that,' as he lowered his eyes to look at his notes. He asked me to point out, on a map of Sofia, the park where I slept on a bench, but I'd never been trained to read a map and couldn't find it. I did remember the name of the park, though, and he found it on the map."

When Kolev couldn't answer those questions the interrogator smiled, leaned back and offered Kolev a cigarette.

"My departure from Sofia came next, and almost step by step he went through the trip to the border area and my crossing, and he jotted down almost everything I said. He asked the times I got the rides, but without a watch I had no way of keeping track of time and told him so. He asked me to show on a map my route to the border, but that was impossible, because I didn't know exactly where I was. When I said that, he smiled again, shook my hand and said, 'If you had been sent here, you'd know the answers to those questions because you would have been trained to memorize them.' After I described how I crossed the border fence, he thanked me for my cooperation and sent me back to my cell. That was the last interrogation session—with him."

"He was satisfied with your answers?" Markov asked.

"I guess so. Why not? I didn't have anything to hide, and told him what I knew, and didn't try to tell things I didn't know."

"Well," Markov said, "it's obvious he used those questions not only to obtain information, but also to see if you were telling the truth. Perhaps what you told him wasn't important, but it could be checked against what he had learned from other escapees. If he caught you lying, God knows what might have happened."

Kolev nodded and raised both hands palms up. "Who knows?" he said. "Look what did happen."

"If that was your last interrogation session with him, what happened then?" Markov asked, ignoring Kolev's last comment.

"Nothing for a while. My daily routine was the same: an hour in the courtyard; the food didn't vary much, and I was allowed to shower once a week. One time a doctor came to the cell and examined me. He didn't ask questions, but looked me over, down my throat, in my ears, and he pointed a small light in my eyes. Once a week an officer came to my cell to inspect it. I always stood when he entered, but he never spoke to me. He just looked around quickly and left. It was boring. I had nothing to read, and it was very quiet, but once I heard what sounded like people struggling in the hall. A cell door opened and closed several times, and I heard yelling and sounds like people falling or fighting. I guess there was some problem with a refugee. I asked the interrogator what had happened, but he didn't answer.

"Finally, one evening, long after the last meal, the guard took me to an interrogation room again. There the Greek interrogator told me our sessions were completed, that his government had no further interest in talking to me. He said, 'I wish you good luck.' I asked if I'd soon be going to a refugee camp for resettlement, and he said, 'Perhaps, but other people want to talk with you first.' I asked who these other people were, and what they wanted to talk with me about. 'The Americans want to talk to you,' he said. That surprised me, so I asked him why Americans would want to talk with me. He said the Greeks worked very closely with the Americans, and the Americans wanted to be satisfied about everything he had reported about me. 'Who knows,' he said, 'you may end up in America.'"

Kolev clenched his fist in front of his chest and said, "I wish now I'd never heard of America."

Chapter 4

Kolev said he had remained in his cell the next day, and no one arrived except those bringing his meals. He was not taken to the courtyard for exercise.

"That evening, rather late—I was getting ready to go to bed—a guard took me to an interrogation room where two men were waiting. Both were dressed in dark, three-piece suits, with white shirts and ties. They stood, shook hands, and spoke to me in Bulgarian.

"The taller one said, 'We are Americans and we wish to welcome you to Greece. We have read the reports of your talks with the Greeks and have discussed with them their impressions of you.'

"Thank you," I said, "I did my best to answer all the questions the Greeks asked me. I hope they believe that."

"They do," the shorter one said. "And we do also. You have been very cooperative."

I didn't have much choice, I thought, but didn't say anything.

"The shorter one said they, too, would like to talk with me, and hoped I would be willing to spend some time with them. I, of course, said it was okay with me. They were very polite."

"They both spoke Bulgarian?" Markov asked.

"Yes, the tall one had an accent and was not fluent, but the short one was a Bulgarian."

"He was a Bulgarian?"

"Yeah, or maybe I should say he had been a Bulgarian. He was obviously a native-speaking Bulgarian. In fact he spoke in the clipped manner of a Bulgarian army officer, but he and the American spoke to each other in English."

"Tell me about them."

"Well, the Bulgarian was, I would guess, in his mid-thirties. He was of medium height and weight, nice looking and spoke as if he were well-educated. He certainly was well-dressed. The American was in his thirties also, perhaps a little younger than the Bulgarian."

"And really, the American spoke Bulgarian also?"

"Yeah, well, he seemed to understand everything I said, and I could understand him, but he spoke Greek better. They both spoke Greek very well, and they sounded like Greeks when they spoke to the Greeks."

"What else do you know about them?"

"I spent hundreds of hours with them over the next five months or so, but didn't learn anything about them. We became friendly, but they never gave me their names, never referred to each other by name, didn't say where they were from, or whether they were married—nothing. Whenever I asked them about themselves, they changed the subject.

"Our service asked many questions about them, but I could only provide their descriptions, how they trained me and what they told me to do. Our service probably thought I was withholding information, but I wasn't.

"And, oh, well, that's long in the past. I described the Bulgarian to you. The American was tall and slender, dark hair, blue eyes. He wore a ring on his right hand, which our service told me was a university ring. I guess the Americans get a ring to wear when they graduate from a university. But I couldn't read what was written on it. He knew a lot about weapons and map and compass reading, and he was always polite and considerate. But I don't know more about him."

"Okay, let's leave that subject. Go on."

"Well, the tall American told me that a young man like me could find many good opportunities in the western world. He said that in the West people can choose the type of work they want to do, live where they want and say what they want without being afraid of the government."

Markov pushed his chair back and stood. "Kolev," he said, "I'm thirsty, would you like some water?"

"Yeah, that would be good," Kolev responded. "And do you mind if I take another cigarette?"

"Not at all," Markov said. He opened the door and told the guard to bring water. While waiting, Markov strode slowly around the room, his hands clasped behind his back. In a few minutes the guard entered and placed a bottle of water and two glasses on the desk. Markov thanked the guard and poured water for them both, and watched as Kolev took several large gulps from his glass. Very gently, he patted Kolev on the shoulder as he returned to his chair.

"Please continue," he said, taking a small sip from his glass.

"Well, the Americans had brought a large paper bag with them. The Bulgarian-American opened it and took out a cold bottle of wine, three glasses and a paper package holding feta cheese and olives. He opened the bottle and poured each of us a glass."

Kolev said the American spread out the paper and told Kolev to help himself. They ate with their fingers.

"The cheese was good, but the wine was awful. It tasted like turpentine. I got used to it during my time in Greece, but the wine has resin in it; they call it 'retsina.' Hundreds of years ago, they said, the Greeks used to seal their wine barrels with resin. The wine took on some of the flavor of the resin, and the Greeks liked the flavor, but it took me time to get used to it.

"The evening was pleasant. The Americans didn't interrogate me. They asked why and how I escaped, but their questions were just part of a friendly chat."

Kolev paused, took a deep drag on his cigarette and blew a stream of smoke toward the ceiling. He continued looking at the ceiling for a moment gathering his thoughts.

Kolev said they told him the Bulgarian would meet with him in a couple of days because the Americans had an agreement that the Greeks would interrogate all refugees first. The Greeks started by questioning the refugees for any information about Bulgaria of interest to their analysts. When that phase of questioning was completed, the refugee was examined for signs that he was not a legitimate refugee, but one who had been sent to the West on a mission for the Bulgarian Intelligence Service. If the Greeks believed the refugee wasn't sent, he was turned over to the Americans for interrogation. The Americans did as the Greeks, and looked for information of interest to their analysts.

Sometimes the Americans, using their own sources and methods, uncovered Bulgarian agents who had slipped past the Greeks as refugees. When that happened, the Americans turned the refugees over to the Greeks. They didn't tell Kolev what the Greeks did with those people.

Kolev sat up straight, looked directly into Markov's eyes, and said, "I assured them that I had not been sent to Greece on a mission for anyone, and they told me the Greeks believed I was an honest young man, looking only for a new future. And, they said, they had no reason to doubt that. After our meeting, I was returned to my cell."

Markov noticed that Kolev was trying hard to convince him that the Americans and the Greeks had believed him during the interrogations. He wondered why Kolev thought this important. His story was so simple, so lacking in intrigue, there was nothing to lie about.

"Kolev?" Markov asked, "did you ever lie to the Americans or the Greeks about your background?"

"No, sir, I didn't lie to them. Well—not about my background—but about being willing to work for the Americans, yes. But I'll tell you about that."

"Have you lied to me about any of this?" Markov asked.

"Lied to you? Heavens no! Why would I lie to you, Mister Markov?" Kolev asked, his voice rising.

"Okay, then, just go on with your story."

"Yes, sir. Well, nothing happened for two days. Then during the evening of the third day I was taken to an interrogation room where the Bulgarian was waiting. He questioned me about some of the same information I had discussed with the Greek, but he didn't care about so many details. He asked me very little about the collective, and showed no interest in my uncle, you know, the one who worked for the Communist Party. We talked about my military service, but when I told him about being assigned to a tank unit, he seemed to know as much about the type of tanks we had as I did and didn't show any interest in them. He wanted to make sure that I knew as much about the tanks as I should. He didn't ask any questions about our training exercise in Czechoslovakia.

"Then he asked something that surprised me. 'Do you know a Lieutenant Colonel Georgi Todorov?' I had to think for a few minutes—then I remembered. I said I knew of a Lieutenant Colonel Todorov in my regiment, but didn't remember his first name. The Bulgarian asked what duties that man had. I said an officer by that name was an intelligence officer attached to my regiment. Sometimes he would call in members of my unit and question them about their families, or what they had said to other people about our unit and its responsibilities, and such things. Todorov questioned one sergeant about why the sergeant's father had refused to join the Communist Party. Sometimes soldiers called to his office never returned to the unit. People were afraid to be called in by him."

"'That's the man,' the Bulgarian said. 'Were you ever called to his office?' No I was not, I told him, but I knew what he looked like, because we saw him walking around our area sometimes."

Leaning back, Kolev glanced at the ceiling, then at Markov, knowing what the next question would be.

"Was that the truth?" Markov asked. "Were you ever called in by this Todorov?"

"No, I told the Americans the truth. But once Todorov called in one of my friends and questioned him about me. That worried me because I had never talked against the Communist Party, or the army or anything like that. I didn't tell the Americans about that.

"Then the Bulgarian asked me if I knew a man named Grigor Lukanov. I knew that name. He was the chief of security police in Plovdiv. Everybody knew about him, and even people outside the collective talked about him. Everyone was really afraid of him because he had people put in prison or even killed for little or nothing. 'He never came to our collective,' I said."

Kolev remembered the Bulgarian was looking at notes on a pad in front of him, then suddenly jerked his head up and said, "I didn't ask you if he came to your collective; I asked you if you knew him."

But Kolev said he told him that he didn't know people in such high positions and the Bulgarian asked no further questions about Lukanov.

The Bulgarian did, as the Greek had done, ask detailed questions about how Kolev had escaped, and he also looked up in a book something about the train Kolev had taken from Plovdiv to Sofia, and the hostel where he stayed.

Kolev wrinkled his brow, his scarred left eye almost closing. He stared at the floor and half-mumbled, "How do you think the Americans knew about Todorov and Lukanov?"

"I presume," Markov said, "the Americans got such information from interrogations by the Greeks of other escapees. Who knows? They probably had agents in Bulgaria, but that's of no interest to us now. Please go on, I'm interested in how the Americans treated you, and why they thought you would spy for them."

"Well, they thought I would spy for them, but I had no such intention, and I'll prove to you I never did."

"Okay, go ahead."

Kolev thought for a moment. He wanted to be very careful how he explained his involvement with the Americans. Where to start?

"From the very beginning," he said, "the American interrogation was different from the Greek interrogation. The Greeks wanted detailed information about everything, but the Americans seemed to know so much about so many things, or had no interest, and most of their questions were about things I said I knew something about. Not much else."

He said the Americans talked to him about three times a week for two weeks, and then did not see him for several weeks.

"They didn't talk to me for a long time, and I began to worry about my future for the first time since I escaped."

"Why?" Markov asked.

"It was just a feeling. The whole thing was taking too long. I wasn't anybody important, I'd never done anything political, had answered every question the Greeks and Americans asked me, and hadn't lied. But how many weeks had it been? I was still locked in a cell. I wanted to get out. I had no appetite, and sent many meals back untouched. I was homesick. I had no one to talk to except American or Greek interrogators. I wondered who would hire me in the West. How do you ask for a job, and what you are expected to do if you don't speak the language? Who would explain it to me? I'm not very smart, just a tractor mechanic on a collective farm. Maybe my father was right. How would I ever learn English, or French or German? It would take me years. I began to think that it was a mistake to escape from Bulgaria."

Kolev smiled at Markov, but his eyes made it a sad smile. He clasped his hands behind his head, looked at the ceiling and mumbled something Markov couldn't understand. He puts his hands in his lap, and looking at them, said, "It's tough to be locked up. I'm not an animal.

"Outside, birds were calling, and although the window was high, wisps of warm breezes blew in during the days, and I could feel the coolness at night. The smell of pine trees reminded me of home. I wept often.

"One evening the guard brought me my meal. It was beans again. When the guard left, I threw it at the cell door. The bowl broke in many small pieces, and the beans splattered against the door and the wall. I yelled, 'Take your damned beans and let me out of here!' Then I threw the water glass against the wall. Moments later the cell door opened and a guard entered and saw the mess. He yelled at me and pushed me against the wall, and then left. After a few minutes the door opened again, and a sergeant came in, carrying a club. Two guards with rifles came in behind him. When the sergeant saw what I had done, he whacked me on the shoulder with the club. The blow spun me around. He hit me again, this time on the back, so hard that it drove me against the wall across the room, where I went down. Then he kicked me in the side and everything went black. When my head cleared I was sitting on my bunk and the sergeant was gone. One of the guards with a rifle was standing over me and another guard had brought a bucket of water, a mop and some rags. The one with the rifle motioned for me to get up and clean up the mess. I stood up, but was very dizzy, and thinking I was going to vomit, sat down again. The guard with the rifle slapped me in the face and made me get up and clean everything up. Afterwards I lay on the bed and slept until a guard returned just before dawn and made me get up and make my bunk.

"They brought me nothing to eat or drink that entire day. It really hurt to move. The following day they again brought me three meals—the first one was beans."

One evening, a week or so after the beating, a guard came to Kolev's cell and took him to an interrogation room where the Americans were waiting. Kolev had no visible bruises and the Americans didn't know Kolev had been beaten. Kolev didn't mention it. The Americans said they had come to discuss Kolev's future. Kolev had grinned broadly, thinking; *surely now I will be leaving for the refugee camp.*

After general conversation about different cultures and lifestyles in various countries in the West, the taller American began a discussion of the political situation in the world. He told Kolev that the West and the Communist world were locked in a deadly struggle, and although people referred to this struggle as a "Cold War," there was another war going on beneath the surface, a war that the populations of both sides were largely unaware. This, he explained, was the clandestine struggle for information about the intentions and capabilities of the other side. He said Kolev undoubtedly agreed that no one in the world wanted a nuclear war to break out because the West had misinterpreted the intentions or actions of the Soviet Union and the Warsaw Pact.

Kolev said he nodded but didn't say anything.

The American continued that many in the West had made great sacrifices, including offering their lives, to ensure that the West was able to meet any challenge made by the Soviet Union and its allies. Not to be able to do that, he said, might encourage the Soviets to be more aggressive, possibly leading to confrontations which could escalate out of control, leading to the very war scenario every thinking person wanted to avoid.

"I said I didn't know of such things, but hoped neither side made such mistakes, and that once resettled in the West I'd work hard at any job I could get, and do whatever possible to be a good citizen. I told them politics wasn't something people where I came from cared or thought about. I was certain, I said, that educated and experienced people on both sides followed such matters, and that was good.

"The American said I shouldn't be so humble, that I was a bright and thoughtful person who had much to offer. And, he said, many people who seek a new life in the free world, like me, were expected to do their part in making that world safer. They're given the opportunity to contribute, to earn their way to the West.

"What do these people do?" I asked.

"'Ivan,' the American said, 'we have a job for you. Once you do it, you will immediately be settled in any non-Communist country you choose—and with our backing.'

"Well, I certainly need a job, but you must know a tractor mechanic can't do anything to help in such serious matters," I said, hoping the American was joking. But he wasn't. "Please," I said, "just let me to go to some country to find a decent job and be like every normal person, with a wife and family. That's why I escaped from Bulgaria, not to find out anything about a Cold War, or any other war."

"'Ivan,' the American continued, 'we want you to go back to Bulgaria for us—just for a few days. And then you'll be free to go wherever you wish.'

"Go back to Bulgaria!" I shouted. "That's crazy. I just escaped from there. I would be arrested and put in prison, maybe even shot or hanged, or whatever they do to such people. In fact there may not be any such people. I never heard of someone escaping and then going back! What you ask is insane."

Kolev's eyes danced and he waived his arms in the air. Markov was amused that Kolev became so agitated in recounting that conversation. He chuckled, but caught himself, and said, "Excuse me, I'm not laughing at you, but you really acted out well your shock at the American's suggestion."

"Hell, I'm not acting! Just look at what that conversation cost me."

"I know, I know, Kolev," Markov interrupted, "but please go on."

"Yeah, well, the American waited until I calmed down. Then he said, 'You'll be in Bulgaria only five days, and you won't be caught. We'll train you for months and help you cross the border. You won't meet anyone inside Bulgaria and you'll be so well trained that no one will ever know you were there. You'll go in at night, and come out at night.'

"What would I do in Bulgaria?" I asked.

"'We'll discuss that when the time comes for you to go,' he said. And he told me that if I agreed to do the job, they would take me out of the interrogation center and let me live in a house until I left to go back to Bulgaria.

"I said there was no way they could convince me to do what they were asking, and demanded to be released from the interrogation center and allowed to go to the refugee camp for resettlement. The Greeks promised me that if I told them the truth, I said, and I had done that."

Kolev pushed his chair back and stood up. He walked to the door, turned and walked back to his chair, putting both hands on the back, and said, "You won't believe what he said next."

"Try me," Markov said.

Kolev pulled the chair back, sat and said "Well, that damned American said that was no longer possible. He said that if I didn't agree to return to Bulgaria for that mission, the Greeks had decided to return me to Bulgaria as an undesirable refugee."

"But why?" I asked. "I've done nothing wrong. I've done everything asked of me. Why would the Greeks send me back to Bulgaria?

"The American said the Greeks thought I should do something to prove that I would be a loyal citizen of a country in the West. They believed, he said, that I should do this mission to earn my way to resettlement, but also, after the mission, I should receive special treatment."

Kolev banged both hands on the desk and leaned toward Markov. "There you have it!" he said. "That's how they treat people. But they didn't care. The American said they would give me three days to think about their offer. If I agreed to go on the mission, they would take me out of the center and start training me. If I chose to reject the mission, the Greeks would take over. They offered to shake hands before they left, but I refused to lift my hand. A guard took me back to my cell.

"Back in the cell, I wondered what to do. I hated the Greeks and the Americans. If I didn't do what the Americans wanted, and the Greeks sent me back, my government would put me in prison, or maybe they would do something worse. To accept might mean being killed, or if caught, executed as a spy. There had been articles in Bulgarian newspapers that people had been executed for being spies. I had made a terrible mistake—what a helluva mess. I should never have left Bulgaria, my life was not good there, but it was never threatened. At least there was a job and my parents, and for the first time, I missed my father and wished I could ask him what to do."

Kolev said he was kept in his cell for the three days he was given to decide, except for the one hour each day in the courtyard and times when he was taken to the bathroom. Nothing changed.

By the evening of the second day he had decided what to do. He would agree to go on the mission, and after entering Bulgaria, immediately turn himself in and tell the Bulgarian authorities everything that had happened to him.

"That way they couldn't accuse me of being a spy, and I'd be helping my government by reporting what the Americans were doing against Bulgaria. They might punish me for escaping, but at least they'd take into consideration that I had turned myself in. Once I made the decision, I was greatly relieved, and that night slept soundly.

"Late on the third day, I was taken to an interrogation room, and there the Americans waited. We had a light conversation for a few minutes, and we smoked and talked about many things—except why they were there. Finally, the American asked if I had reached a decision.

"When I told them I was prepared to prove myself worthy of migrating to the West, and to prove my loyalty by going on the mission, they were really happy. They shook my hand and patted me on the back. Then the Bulgarian opened a drawer and took out a bottle of whisky and glasses and poured each of us a big drink. We clinked glasses, making toasts to the future. We drank for a long time. I had drunk whiskey only a couple of times before, and it wasn't long before I became quite tipsy, but we had a good time and laughed and told jokes.

"One story the American told was about a refugee who had escaped and had brought a donkey with him. He said they wanted to find out how the guy had managed to cross the border with a donkey. When they brought the refugee there, to the center, the Americans met with him and asked him why he had escaped, and why he had brought a donkey. The refugee, an uneducated man from a very poor village, explained that some years earlier the Communists had taken his small plot of land, plus his house, and put it into a collective farm. So he was angry that he then had to work on a collective. He also had a small flock of sheep, and they took them too, but left him a donkey he had had for years. Several years later they moved another family into his house, and his family had to share the house. The family had four children, and the house had only two bedrooms. That year, he said, he was notified to turn his donkey over to the collective, and he said he would be damned if he would do that, so he escaped—with the donkey. The American said they asked him where the donkey was then, and the man answered, 'Hell, I don't know, the Greeks took it when I crossed the border.'

"We all roared with laughter.

"The American also said that a boy of sixteen had escaped the year before. When they finished talking to him at the center they decided to send him to the refugee resettlement camp with a request that some family be found to take the boy in. When they met with the boy the night before he was to leave, they asked him where he would like to resettle. The boy said he would like to go to Czechoslovakia. When they told him that Czechoslovakia was a Communist country, the boy said, 'Oh! Then I'll go to Yugoslavia.' We roared with laughter again.

"Late in the night, we separated. A guard took me back to my cell, and he was kind enough to take my arm and help me down the hall. The next day nothing happened, but the day after, about mid-morning, a guard came and took my towel, razor and soap. About an hour later the guard returned and led me down the hall and outside to the front of the center. Waiting for me was a military jeep and the Bulgarian, who told me to get in the back. A driver drove us out to the coast road, and we turned south for several kilometers before coming to a farmhouse on the left, about a hundred meters or so from the road. We drove to that house on a dirt path and got out. Signs were posted at the edge of the property that read, I later found out, 'Danger, Mines!'

"From that moment on, I was in the hands of the CIA."

Chapter 5

"We walked to the back of the house. What a place. It was right on the beach at the end of a small cove that opened to the Aegean. On both sides, extending to the mouth of the cove, were cliffs a couple of hundred meters high. A small island sat in the middle of the cove about a hundred meters from the shore.

A large patio covered by a grape arbor extended the width of the back of the house. In the shade of the arbor were several chairs, a small table and a man waiting. He spoke to me in Bulgarian, shook hands, and showed us into the house."

"He spoke to you in Bulgarian?" Markov asked.

"Yeah, he was a Macedonian Greek about fifty or sixty years old. He wouldn't tell me how old he was, even though I lived with him for over eight months."

But during those months, Kolev learned the man had been a Greek guerrilla, fighting with a large band against the Germans and Bulgarians occupying Greece during World War II. He had also fought against the Greek Communists during the Greek civil war, after World War II. He had no family. They had all been killed in one of those wars.

"The Americans were taking care of him. He didn't tell me that, but it was obvious. That old man and the Americans liked each other very much, and they laughed and joked together whenever they came to the house. He was the toughest man I ever met, and could walk up and down those mountains around Kavalla for hours without stopping. He didn't need water and never seemed to need to rest. He didn't talk much, and we could be together for hours without a word being spoken."

Kolev stood up and held his right hand just below his shoulder. "He was shorter than I am, and came up to about here on me, but he was stocky and strong."

He smiled and sat on the edge of his chair. He obviously enjoyed talking about this man. "His face was darkly browned and wrinkled from the sun, particularly around his eyes, and he had a big black moustache, flecked with gray, which matched his hair. I really learned to like him. When he smiled at you his whole face smiled, and his teeth were so white, but, Mister Markov, he was a man you wouldn't want to have as an enemy.

"They called him 'Petros,' and they introduced me to him as 'Vangeli.' I'm sure the Americans never told either of us the other's true name."

The house had one large room, Kolev said, and at one end was an old tan sofa, two chairs and a small coffee table resting on a white flokati throw rug. The rest of the beige-tiled floor was bare. In the middle was a large table with four chairs under a green-shaded light, hanging from the ceiling. At the other end of the room was a small cooking stove, cabinets for dishes and glasses, and a small box that Kolev couldn't identify. Nothing hung on the whitewashed walls except an icon, which Petros had said belonged to him. The ambiance was bright, cheerful austerity. On each side of the door a large window looked out on the cove. At the front of the house, the side facing the road, were two small bedrooms, with a bathroom between them, and that side had neither windows nor a door. The house was clean, and Kolev had never been inside such a fine house.

"Petros took me to one of the bedrooms which had a bed, a chair and hooks on the back of the door to hang things. On the bed new clothes were laid out: two pairs of khaki trousers, three shirts, underwear, socks, and a bathing suit, sandals and a pair of military boots. Also they gave me a brown sweater, a military-type field jacket, two towels, a razor and several bars of soap. That was the most clothing I had had since I was in the army, and they all fit. The house had no heating of any kind, but two thick, wool army blankets were on the bed.

"Petros served us all a mid-day meal, and after we had eaten the American told me that I was never to leave the house without Petros, that Petros would be with me every minute I lived there. He said I could swim when I wanted, and not worry that unauthorized people might visit the house. No one would come near the cliffs on either side of the cove, he said, so no strangers would ever see me at this house. In a few days, my training program would begin, and he said they'd teach me map and compass reading, care and use of weapons, how to prepare reports, and photography. He explained that during my stay I'd get physical endurance training, and that we would work together often during the day, but also train at night. He said they would give me a Greek identification card, but that I should never show that card to anyone unless told to do so by Petros. Then the Americans left.

"Petros showed me that the small box in the cooking area was where he kept food cold so it wouldn't spoil. I knew the army had such boxes, and the collective had a large one, but I had never seen one in a house before. You didn't need to put ice in it, because electricity made it stay cold. He told me that there would always be food, including fresh fruit, cold water, juices and sometimes beer in the box, and that he would prepare all our meals. Whenever I wanted something to drink or a piece of fruit, I could help myself from the box. I had to make my bed and sweep my room every day, and we would take turns sweeping the large room and cleaning the bathroom. Once a week, he said, someone would bring food to the house. We would each do our own laundry in the bathroom."

In the afternoon Petros and Kolev had gone swimming. They swam to the rock island, and Kolev had been surprised to find that there were hundreds of mussels attached to rocks at the water line. They lay on the rocks, looking at the puffs of white clouds, and picked and ate mussels. Kolev recalled that he became tired swimming to the rocks, but Petros had been a strong swimmer.

"But, by the time I left there," Kolev said, "swimming to the rocks and back was easy for me. It was very pleasant living in that house. I could have lived there forever. The training was not as pleasant.

"Two days later, in the afternoon, the Bulgarian came to the house. He had several maps of northern Greece and for several hours we sat at the table in the large room and he taught me to read what was on the maps. When he started, Petros left the house, and every time the Americans came to the house to talk and train me, Petros always went outside or to his bedroom. That day the Bulgarian taught me about the scale of a map, what that scale meant about the size of things on a map and how to read the symbols on the margins.

"He showed that from the map I could learn where I was, where I wanted to go and how long it would take to get there.

"Are you interested in how they trained me, Mister Markov? Maybe you don't care about these details."

Markov rose and walked around the desk. He took two cigarettes from the pack and lit them, handing one to Kolev. Returning to his chair, he sat and said, "No, its okay. I want to know something about your training. It's an indication of how serious the Americans viewed you, and what they were training you to do. Please go on."

"Well, the Bulgarian taught me how the scale of the map would indicate distances between objects. We used a one-to-fifty-thousand scale map, so that makes one kilometer on the ground equal about twenty millimeters on the map. We spent a great deal of time learning about contour lines, and he showed how they measure heights, both valleys and mountain peaks, and how steep or flat the terrain is. It was interesting—just by looking at a map you can tell all that."

Kolev propped an elbow on the desk and rested his forehead in his hand. He paused, trying to remember, and said, "Oh, yeah—one more thing—maps have certain distances between contour lines and these distances can easily be figured out. For example, if you are standing on terrain one thousand meters above sea level, and the peak of a ridge in front of you is two thousand meters above sea level, and there are five contour lines between where you are and the peak, that means that there are two hundred meters on the ground between each line."

Kolev said that after a few days of map training in the house, the Bulgarian took him to the mountains to the west and showed him land features. There he taught Kolev how to orient the map to find where he was by looking at land features in the distance and locating them on the map. They did that for several consecutive days. On those occasions, the Bulgarian would arrive at the house in a jeep and drive Petros and Kolev into the mountains, and often there were no roads, or even a path to follow.

"That jeep could drive over very rough and steep terrain. They were better than our Russian-made jeeps," Kolev said.

"Were there any markings on the jeep? Was there a license plate?" Markov asked.

"No, and I looked for that. There never were markings or license plates on any vehicle that came to the house. Since I had decided to tell our authorities about everything I knew, I tried to see and remember as much as I could, but they were very careful. In fact, once a week a Greek driver—and there were several different ones—came to the house to pick up a list of the food items we needed for the coming week, and returned a few hours later with the food. The drivers used different jeeps, but none had any markings, not even serial numbers or unit designations, and the drivers never spoke to me or used any names."

"Okay, go on with your training," Markov said, trying to conceal a yawn behind the palm of his hand.

"Well, after studying maps and going out to compare the maps with terrain features many times, the Bulgarian had me study a map and then draw a sketch of what land features I would see if we were located at a certain place on the map.

After about a month of map training, I became pretty good at reading maps—or at least the Bulgarian told me that."

"A full month of studying maps seems to be a long time on that one subject," Markov observed.

"Yeah, well we didn't do that every day. The Bulgarian came to train me about three times a week. When we worked in the house, he would usually come late in the afternoon, and when we went out to study terrain in the mountains, it was usually for about a half a day. I had the impression the Bulgarian had other things he was working on, because he always seemed very busy, and in a hurry to teach me what he had planned for that day and to leave."

"How often did the American come to see you," Markov asked.

"Well, I think he came to the house by himself about once a week. He would observe the training, if the Bulgarian were there, and ask me questions about what I had learned. He often also spent time questioning me about how I was doing personally, and he seemed concerned that I was content with the way I was living. He asked about our food, about how I spent my free time, and twice in the first month or so he went swimming with Petros and me. We swam to the rocks each time, and there we rested and talked and then swam back. During those times he also asked me questions about my family; why my father and I were not very close, what kind of woman my mother was, and how she got along with my father. He also asked if I was a good hunter, whether I had experience shooting weapons and what kind of future I saw for myself. He asked a lot of questions—not as an interrogator, but just in normal conversation. For example, he wanted to know why I never talked about my grandparents. He was the first person to ask me about my grandparents, except for their names, and when and where they were born. I didn't know my grandparents, but I remembered that once, when I was very young, the parents of my father came to visit us and that they had come a great distance. But they both died shortly after that. My mother's father was killed when the Communists took over Bulgaria, and who knows whether he was on the Communist side or the Royalist, because we never talked about him. My mother's mother came to visit us at times. She worked in the rose fields in central Bulgaria, and I didn't like her very much because she was always complaining about something. My mother wasn't very happy when she came. When I was in Greece I didn't know whether she was still alive, because we hadn't talked about her for years before I escaped."

Markov leaned back, clasped his hands behind his head and stared at Kolev for a long moment, frowning. Kolev raised his eyebrows and shrugged. "I don't know why he cared about my grandparents," he said. "I didn't ask him to ask about them. Perhaps he was just being polite by showing interest in my family. Who knows?"

"Yes, of course," Markov said. "But I'm sure he was sorry he asked. Please go on."

"Well, early one morning a Greek driver arrived, and Petros told me to put my boots on. After I did that—it was the first time I'd worn them—we got in the jeep and drove to the foot of a mountain that rose gradually to the west. The driver let us out and left. Petros said we were to start getting me into good physical condition. I thought I was in good condition, but I must tell you, Mister Markov, by the end of that day I thought Petros was going to walk me to death. We began going up the side of that tall mountain. It was not steep, a gradual incline, but it seemed to go up forever. We climbed about two hours, and Petros' pace never slackened. My legs ached and were shaky, and my breath came in gasps, but Petros wasn't even breathing hard. He had brought water in a canteen, and he finally stopped and let me drink, and I told him I couldn't go on without resting. So he gave me ten minutes—I was thinking more about an hour. While I lay on my back, trying to recover, he didn't even sit. When the resting time was up, we started again, and while it was not a terribly hot day, my shirt was completely wet and my trousers were soaked almost to my knees. Within ten minutes after getting up, I was breathing hard again and was having a difficult time putting one foot in front of the other. Petros continued without changing the pace; he didn't speak or look back, but kept walking. Soon I became dizzy, then I vomited, and sat on the ground. Petros came and stood over me, waiting, looking at me."

Kolev ran a hand over his hair and then placed it on his knee, nodding his head, as if remembering the day clearly. He smiled slightly and said, "After a few minutes, Petros gave me a lecture. He said we weren't just conditioning my body, but my mind as well, because when the body gets tired, the mind tells us to quit. We must learn to ignore what the mind tells us, and push on beyond what we think our physical limits are. We can always do more than we think. Many men had died, he said, because they had given in to what their minds told them, while men physically weaker had survived great ordeals because they had tough minds and strong spirit. 'Now get up!' he said. I did, and we continued climbing.

"After perhaps a total of four hours climbing, Petros turned south and we began walking down an incline. About a thousand meters farther we came to a small stand of trees, and there was the Greek driver, sitting in the jeep. We returned to the house."

Back at the house, he said, Petros told him to drink all the water he wanted. After Kolev bathed and changed his clothes, he discovered that he had two blisters on his left foot, and one was bleeding. He said he told Petros, who poured alcohol on both of them. It burned terribly, and Kolev howled and cursed Petros, who laughed, seeming to enjoy the occasion. Petros sprinkled both with white powder and covered them with gauze. Kolev slept until he was called for dinner.

"We had not eaten since breakfast and I was hungry. As we ate, Petros said nothing about the day, but he seemed melancholy, lost in his own thoughts. A couple of days earlier the Greek driver had brought us a radio and a bottle of what the Greeks call ouzo. It's like our mastika. After dinner, Petros turned on the radio, opened the bottle and poured us both a drink."

In the middle of their second drink, Petros had lit a cigarette, turned the radio up to full volume, the music filling the room with the beat of the orient, and the high-pitched sounds of the *bouzouki*. He sat for a moment, his head cocked, then he rose, as if hypnotized by the music, and drawn by the call of centuries of Greek culture to sooth a troubled soul in an ancient ritual of dance. Moving almost imperceptibly to the rhythm, he bent forward from the waist, then slowly turned his upper body to the right, and straightened, extending his arms as if they were wings. Moving around the room, turning slowly, he abruptly dropped, squatting almost to the floor, turning slowly on one foot, his other leg extended. He straightened, and still turning, made a little jump, raised one leg and struck his foot with one hand. Arms still outstretched, his head fell back, almost looking at the ceiling, the cigarette dangling from his lips. He continued around the room, clicking his fingers to the beat. He was oblivious of Kolev, his eyes unfocused. Several times, in a low guttural voice, he shouted, '*Opa!*' and twice he emitted a shrill whistle. With perspiration glistening on his face, he suddenly stopped. Without a word he turned off the radio, refilled his glass and went to the veranda, where he sat and gazed out to the sea.

"I left him there and went to bed. I said nothing, because I didn't think he wanted me to.

"The next day my legs were very sore, but Petros and I swam out to the rocks and ate mussels. The salt water burned my blisters, but by the end of the day they were better. In the afternoon, the American came. Petros talked to him in Greek and apparently told him of our hike the day before, because when he finished the American asked to see my blisters, and said that we would not have another hiking exercise until they were healed. And after that, he said, we would start a regular hiking program. Smiling, he said it would take me some weeks, but I would soon find that I was as tough as Petros. He was wrong."

During the few days of cessation in the hiking, the Bulgarian had come twice. He went over all the things he had taught Kolev about map reading, and then from a briefcase he often carried, he removed a dark green, military hand-held compass.

"I'm sure you know what a compass is and how they work, so I won't try to tell you a lot about that," Kolev said.

"I don't know much about a compass," Markov said, "but I'm not sure I care. Should I?"

"No, I guess not, but perhaps I should explain a little, because a compass played a major role in my mission. I'll tell you quickly. The Bulgarian showed me that the compass had a magnetized needle that turned on a pivot. That assembly is enclosed in a case, and you can turn the case to shoot azimuths."

"What's an azimuth?" Markov asked.

"Well, you look through a sight on the compass at an object on the ground, and you can read on the compass the angle, in degrees from north, of a straight line from you to the object. That line is the azimuth, and you could also do it in the dark, because the face of the compass glowed in the dark."

"I understand, but you needn't describe to me more than I need to know about how a compass functions," Markov said, glancing at his watch. "Perhaps it is enough to know that the Americans taught you to work with a compass."

Kolev ran both hands through his hair. He didn't know how this interview with Markov was going to turn out, but he knew, instinctively, that if it went badly for him, Markov must understand precisely how a compass works and how the use of a compass affected his life. His mind raced to think how he might keep Markov's attention on this subject a bit longer.

"All right. I won't say more about how a compass works, but let me explain how I was trained to use one," Kolev said. He paused to see Markov's reaction, but Markov was looking at his notes, so Kolev continued: "The Bulgarian taught me to use a compass, together with a map, and how to travel with just those two things. He started by standing on the patio and showing me the rock island in the middle of the cove on the map, and then showing me with the compass that the azimuth reading from the patio to the island was ninety-four degrees. Almost due East.

"We didn't do any more work with the compass until my blisters healed. Then they'd send Petros and me out at least three days a week. We'd walk three or four hours and then be met by the Greek driver and returned to the house. These walks were very hard for me, because we were climbing most of the time. During the second or third week, we walked over a ridgeline one day and there waiting for us in the jeep were the American and the Bulgarian. I never understood how they knew where to find us, because there were no roads that I could see."

On the hood of the jeep they spread out a map of the area, he said, and showed him how to orient the map and the compass. They told him to locate several mountain peaks on the map and to shoot azimuths at them, then note those azimuths on the map by drawing straight lines with a pencil from their location to the objects.

"More and more frequently they would intercept Petros and me during our hikes, and we would repeat the same exercise. Then one day, not long after we had begun our hike, they stopped us just as the path we were following wound around the side of a steep mountain. They gave me a compass and told me to walk one hour on a course of about two hundred and seventy-eight degrees, and one hour on a course of one hundred ninety degrees. It was something like that. I don't remember the exact headings, but in those directions. There, they said, they would be waiting for us. That was my first chance to do that on my own, and I hoped Petros would know where we were if I made a mistake. Following their instructions, I would shoot an azimuth to an object several hundred meters in front of me, and when we reached that point shoot another azimuth on the same course at another object ahead of me. I went on that way for one hour, and Petros played no role, except to tell me how much time had elapsed. I didn't have a watch yet. Petros would watch me shoot the azimuth and when I pointed out the next object we had to reach, he'd lead me there. At the end of the first hour we arrived at the top of a small knoll. There, as I began to shoot an azimuth to start the second leg of the exercise, we heard a whistle in the distance, and on the side of a hill west of us were the Americans in the jeep. They waved and drove off. We did the second leg as we had done the first, and at the end of the second hour we reached a path at the bottom of a valley. There the Americans were waiting. They congratulated me, and discussed something with Petros in Greek. When they finished, they congratulated me again and said that Petros believed I might make a good cross-border agent if he could get me in good physical condition. I said I thought I was already in good condition, but they laughed, and winked at Petros as we got into the jeep and returned to the house.

"That night, lying in my bed, I thought about the statement that, 'I might become a pretty good cross-border agent.' I was satisfied that I had deceived the Americans well, and realized that all of the physical conditioning was completely unnecessary. When they put me across the border, I intended to turn myself in to the nearest Bulgarian border post, and I didn't need to be in great condition to do that.

"Not long after, Petros and I were hiking in hills next to a long valley. Down in the valley, a long way from us, we saw a hunter with a gun over his shoulder and what appeared to be birds tied to his belt. Petros stopped and whistled to him. The man looked up and Petros turned his hand clockwise pointing it at the hunter with his palm up. I didn't understand what he was doing, but the hunter held up five fingers. He had shot five birds. Petros tried for a month to teach me how to whistle like that, without success."

Kolev paused and stared at the ceiling. After a moment, he clasped both hands behind his head, looked down and cleared his throat. He still remembered the wildness and the beauty of those mountains, and he wanted Markov to know about it; he had an urge to tell him.

"The mountains in that part of Greece are quite barren," he said, "with most of the foliage being low brush. Grass grows on the slopes of some mountains, and wild flowers are everywhere in the spring. But the land is only useful for grazing sheep and goats. We saw many shepherds, usually at a distance."

He and Petros had always tried to avoid the shepherds, but often came upon shelters where the shepherds spent their nights, usually a simple lean-to and a small corral made by stones stacked about one meter high to form a fence. The sheep were put there at night for security because wolves were in the area, and although they would not attack a man, unless he was obviously wounded, the wolves would attack the sheep and goat herds. For protection, the shepherds always had three or four large, vicious dogs that would attack anything that approached too close to the flocks. And they were big enough to attack wolves. The dogs would bark when they heard anything near the flock, so Petros and Kolev had little difficulty avoiding the shepherds, changing direction when they heard the barking.

"Once though, we heard dogs barking on the other side of a ridge. Since we didn't intend to cross that ridge we kept walking, but over the ridge, running directly at us, came three large sheep dogs. They were barking and growling, with their teeth bared, and obviously coming to attack. I started to run, but Petros shouted, 'Stay!' From under his shirt he pulled a pistol and rapidly fired two shots into the ground in front of the dogs. The dogs stopped and retreated a few meters, but continued barking and growling at us. Then the shepherd appeared on top of the ridge and whistled at the dogs, and they ran to him. The shepherd and Petros yelled back and forth until finally they both laughed, and the shepherd and the dogs went back over the ridge. We continued walking."

Markov raised his eyebrows in surprise. "Did Petros always have a gun with him?" he asked.

"I don't know. I was surprised," Kolev answered. "He always wore a shirt loose at the waist when we were hiking, but I didn't know he carried a pistol in his belt. He never said a word about it.

"I asked Petros how the shepherds found food and water, and he said water was plentiful in the mountains, so they always knew where to find it. Food, he said, was brought to them from the shepherd's village about once a week. He explained that the shepherds took the flocks into the mountains in the spring and stayed there all summer, returning to their villages with the flocks in the fall. Every shepherd I saw, and I saw many, wore long capes of sheepskin with the wool turned out. The capes were both warm and waterproof. Although the days could be quite hot, nights in the mountains were cold, and the sheepskin capes were necessary."

Kolev put his left elbow on the arm of his chair and rested his chin on his hand. After a moment of looking at the table he sat back, took two cigarettes from the pack and lit them, handing one to Markov. "I would give anything to see those mountains again," he said.

"Gradually," he continued, "I reached the point where I could walk as fast as Petros on the three- to four-hour hikes, and not be tired when we returned to the house. Then Petros began making the hikes longer, extending them to six hours. That made a big difference, and during the last hour of the longer hikes I was very tired and my legs ached and were shaky. Petros stopped more often the last two hours of the six-hour hikes, but eventually we could walk six hours without stopping.

"One afternoon after we had returned from a hike, the Bulgarian and the American came to the house, and the Bulgarian took from his briefcase a pistol and put it on the table in the large room. They explained to me that it was a Colt forty-five, semi-automatic, and that it was the type used by the American army. They let me hold it and explained how far it could shoot accurately, how much it weighed and how many rounds it would hold. Then they spent over an hour teaching me how to take the pistol apart and put it back together again. When they left, they left the pistol, and told me to practice doing that every day. Petros saw that I did it at least an hour a day, and before long I could do it quickly. They didn't leave any ammunition.

"A week or so later they came again and told me show to them how quickly I could take the pistol apart and put it together again. They were pleased that I did so well. The Bulgarian put the Colt forty-five in his briefcase and took out another pistol and put it on the table. That pistol, he said, was a Browning nine-millimeter. They told me about its weight and range, and showed me that it held fourteen rounds, and then taught me how to take it apart and put it back together again. They left that pistol to practice with as I had the Colt. After a few days I could take that pistol apart and put it back together again as quickly as I could the Colt.

"Some days later, the Americans returned, bringing back the Colt pistol and ammunition for both pistols. We took them outside and walked over to the base of the hill on the right of the cove. Petros came along to watch. That was the first time he came to a training session. The Bulgarian put a round target at the base of the hill about 30 meters from us, while the American taught me how to put shells in the magazine for the Colt. Then, without putting the magazine in the pistol, he showed me how to shoot it. He taught me to spread my legs a little wider than the width of my shoulders, to face the target squarely, to crouch a bit and hold the pistol in front of me with both hands. He told me not to close one eye to aim, the way I'd been taught in the army to aim a rifle, but to aim down the barrel with both eyes open. For some minutes he made me do that over and over again, pulling the trigger each time. When he was satisfied, he put the magazine in and showed me how to put a round in the chamber, explaining that was always to be done with the safety on. He repeated many times that I must never turn away from the target after I had fired, without first putting the safety on. He then told me to fire a round at the target.

"I took the position I had been taught, aimed and fired. I was shocked. The noise was deafening. The pistol recoiled so much that it kicked back almost to my right shoulder. The shot struck about four meters over the target, and the three of them laughed. I turned around to look at them, and when I did, the American hit me hard on my left shoulder. The blow staggered me, and as I started to stumble, he grabbed the pistol and shouted, 'Never turn away from the target after firing without putting the safety on!' I was embarrassed. He had just told me that before I fired. I apologized. He put his arm around my shoulder, telling me that was something I must never forget, no matter what the circumstances, because there was never an acceptable excuse for someone being shot accidentally."

Kolev hung his head, folded his hands on the desk and thought for a few moments. "I should've shot myself," he said, "then I wouldn't be here."

"Well, you didn't," Markov said. Then he chuckled, and said; "Back then you probably would've missed." With that, he tapped his forehead with heels of both hands, winced, and muttered, "I'm sorry. That wasn't funny."

Kolev looked up, smiled, then grinned broadly and said, "Well, actually it was rather funny."

Both men laughed boisterously.

"Please go on," Markov said, wiping his eyes with the back of his sleeve.

"Okay, well, we spent the next hour or so firing the Colt and the Browning," he continued, "but I never hit the target. I liked the Browning better than the Colt, because its recoil was much less and it was not as noisy. Even though I was not accurate, the American said he was pleased with me, so we returned to the house where the Bulgarian taught me how to clean the pistols. They left oil, patches and a short rod and told me to take both weapons apart and clean them thoroughly. When they left, they took the ammunition with them. Petros watched me clean the weapons, and when I finished, he put them both in his bedroom."

Kolev and Petros hiked the next two days, and the following day the Americans arrived again and they held another firing practice. Kolev was better, hitting the target several times with the Browning. The American and the Bulgarian then had made a five-hundred-drachma bet and took turns firing at the target. They each fired three rounds in rapid succession. The American hit the target three times. The Bulgarian hit the middle of the target once, one hit the target left of center and one missed. So the American had won. They returned to the house where they again told Kolev to clean the weapons. But before leaving, the American gave the five hundred drachmas to Petros and told him a driver would come that night, and that Petros was to take Kolev to dinner in the town of Drama.

"After dark the driver arrived in the jeep, and we drove to the small town northwest of Kavalla. On the main square, at a little taverna with only six tables, Petros ordered a fine meal of baby lamb chops, salad and bread. The food was delicious, and we drank retsina wine that was drawn from one of the barrels that lined the walls of the taverna. The Greek driver ate with us, and while he and Petros talked normally in Greek, Petros told me not to talk loudly because he didn't want others in the taverna to hear me speaking Bulgarian.

"After we ate, we sat at a table on the square and drank coffee and brandy and smoked cigarettes. On the way back to the house the driver and Petros sang songs at the top of their lungs. It was a grand evening. I had been in the interrogation center or the house since I arrived in Greece, and it was great to see people and to eat so well. I slept very well that night, and we didn't get up early in the morning, and we didn't hike the next day.

"The following day, the Americans came again for another hour of weapons training. Because I told them I liked the Browning better than the Colt, the

Browning was the only pistol we trained with after that. I was getting better at firing the Browning, and out of every twenty or so rounds, was hitting the target ten to twelve times, and the other shots missed by only a little. I was still firing one round at a time. After the firing, we went into the house where the American explained that we would now start map and compass training at night, and that we would begin the night exercises by dropping Petros and me at a place we would locate on the map before we started. From there they would give me compass headings to follow. There would be several headings in each exercise. The first exercise would be that night. They left.

"After our evening meal, the Americans returned, and at the table they showed me on the map where we would start and the headings. We left in the jeep under a full moon, so once we arrived at the starting point and spread the map on the hood of the jeep, we had no need for a flashlight. They showed me the first objective on the map, and then pointed out a peak on a ridgeline north of us, telling me to shoot an azimuth at it and record it on the map, drawing a pencil line from our position to the peak. I did. It was about two hundred and eighty-six degrees. You know, Mister Markov, this took place some years ago, and I'm not certain of the exact degrees, but that was the general direction, and I developed a pretty good memory for compass headings. I realize the headings aren't important to you, but this will give you a good idea how they trained me, and how thorough they were. In any case, they told me to walk to that ridge using the compass, and from there shoot an azimuth of one hundred thirty-five degrees, then draw a pencil line on the map of that heading. They gave me a small notebook to record that azimuth and the object I sighted on. They told me to follow that heading for one hour and then shoot another heading of one hundred and eighty-five degrees, again drawing that heading on the map and noting it in the notebook. I had to walk on that heading for one hour.

"They left, and Petros and I started walking. I had trouble from the very beginning. I had no trouble shooting the headings, sighting on objects short distances ahead of me, but when we started walking toward the objects I was easily thrown off course if a cloud blocked the moonlight, or if for a few minutes we couldn't see the object. When the moon would reappear, I was often off course by a few degrees. I'd then have to shoot a new azimuth at the peak, draw a new line on the map and make a new entry in the notebook. This went on during the entire exercise, so when we finished the three hours of walking, I had many lines and compass readings on the map, with many entries in the notebook. And we weren't where we were supposed to be, because the Americans weren't there. I explained to Petros where we were; that was easy to find on the map, but didn't know where we were supposed to be. The many headings taken and recorded on the map, and the notebook, took so much time that we had not covered the distance we should have in three hours. Petros then took over, and we walked about a half an hour. He didn't use the map or compass, but walked directly to a deserted shepherd's lean-to, where the Americans were waiting. We returned to the house."

Kolev smiled at Markov and told him how dumb he felt after making so many mistakes. "But back at the house," he said, "the American told me I had done well, and shouldn't worry about the difficulties. They expected that. I thought to myself that needn't worry about the difficulties; because once they put me across the border into Bulgaria I didn't need this training to find a border post.

"For the next several weeks we had three or four night-training exercises a week, and pistol training often—at least four days a week. I was getting pretty good with the pistol and could hit the target six or seven times out of every ten shots. Then they instructed me to fire multiple rounds at the target. They called that rapid fire. We started with three rounds, and eventually I was firing five rounds in rapid succession at the target. In a couple of weeks I became pretty good at that also. I didn't hit the target each time, but the American told me that if I had to fire a weapon during my mission, it would probably be at a soldier armed with an AK-47, and I wouldn't win in such an exchange. My only objective, he explained, was to be able to fire several rounds rapidly and accurately, so that whoever I was facing would duck for cover rather than fire at me. Then I might have a chance to escape."

Kolev recalled that as the map training continued, he had learned to overcome losing sight of an object on the heading he was following by holding the compass in front of him, making certain that the needle continued pointing in the same direction. The Americans told him it wouldn't be totally accurate, but that he should be able to stay close to his course for short distances.

"After that, the night training changed. They no longer gave me objectives and headings to follow, but merely selected a point on the map and told me to go there. They'd drop Petros and me somewhere, and I'd have to use the map to find out where we were, locate the point where I had to go, and determine the headings to get there. To find out where we were, they told me to shoot azimuths at several points of land, and then draw a line on the map from the object I had sighted on, using the reverse of the azimuth. For example, if I shot an azimuth of ninety degrees to an object, I'd draw a line on the map of two hundred seventy degrees from that object. I would do that for each sighting, and where those lines crossed on the map, that would be my location. They instructed me to check my position about every half-hour, and to record in my notebook each object I sighted on and the compass reading to those objects. We trained several weeks doing that, and I became quite accurate finding out where I was and where to go. When we returned to the house, the Americans could take the map and read my notebook and determine exactly where I had been."

Kolev looked for any indication that Markov had realized the significance of what he had just said. But Markov was rubbing his chin and staring at the ceiling.

"While our night-training exercises continued at a rate of four or five outings a week," Kolev continued, "the Bulgarian came often during the days, and began teaching me how to take photographs. He introduced me to a thirty-five-millimeter Leica, and at first we used standard film, which I believe took thirty-five photographs, but later they brought rolls of film that took seventy-two photographs, which they said they had created. The Bulgarian explained how a camera works, and we took photographs around the cove. He set up a darkroom in our bathroom, and, after we shot photographs, we would go to the bathroom to develop them. It was interesting. In this way he showed the effect of sunlight on the object I was photographing. If the sun were shining directly into the camera, we recovered little or nothing. Morning or evening light from behind me, shining on the object, produced the best results.

"After a week or so of that we went up in the hills to practice taking pictures of flowers and bushes up close, and of shepherds in the distance. That's how I learned the range limits of the camera. After I understood that well, we put a long-range lens on the camera; it was remarkable how far you could photograph with that lens. We also took photographs of trucks and cars on a road, which taught me how to change the speed on the camera so that moving objects wouldn't be blurred. After about three weeks of this training, I took rather good photographs under almost all conditions, and I could develop the film myself."

Markov looked at his watch, wondering what he was going to serve his brother to drink that evening if he didn't have time to buy rakia on the way home.

"One afternoon," Kolev continued, "the American arrived and talked to me alone for quite awhile. He went over all my training, explaining that I was then in excellent physical condition, and that Petros had said that physically I was ready for my mission. He went over the things I had learned; how to fire a pistol effectively, how to use a map and compass and how to take photographs. They had nothing more to teach me, but he said they had a moral obligation to prepare me as best they knew how to keep me safe on my mission. He said that throughout my training, he and the Bulgarian, and also Petros, had been evaluating me, and that they had sent my interrogation records from the center, along with their assessments, to Washington. There, he said, a staff of psychologists had reviewed them, and evaluated me as one who was disciplined, conscientious and intelligent. I learned quickly, he said, and adapted easily to change and obstacles. Whether I was prepared mentally for a cross-border mission was a more subjective issue, he said. Petros' assessment of me was important to them, because even though Petros was not a trained observer, he was tough-minded, with much experience, and knew whether a man was a quitter, or couldn't handle stress. Petros, he said, had pushed me to the limits of my endurance during our hiking exercises, and reported that I had developed the mental toughness to accomplish whatever mission they gave me. The American said he was proud of me, and asked how I felt about my upcoming mission, whether after all my training I felt confident about my capabilities. I told him I felt ready, and believed I could accomplish a mission successfully, and that I was not afraid. He said I would be afraid when the time came for my mission, but if I believed I was well trained and had confidence in myself, I could overcome that fear. He then shook hands with me and left.

"I would have told the American anything he wanted to hear. I was tired of the training and anxious to have them send me back to Bulgaria. I had learned a lot about the American training, and by going through all that surely my government would be convinced that I had provided a valuable service and was a loyal Bulgarian. Now there would be new opportunities for a better life in Bulgaria. But look at me, here, after all these years."

Kolev dropped his head and examined his hands. His fists were clinched and the vessels in his forearms bulged.

"Go on with what happened next," Markov said.

"Well, the next day the Bulgarian came and brought masks, snorkels, flippers and two spear guns. Petros taught me how to snorkel, and we practiced near the beach in shallow water. That was a new world for me. To be able to look under the sea at the different types of life, the sand and rock formations was wonderful. Petros also taught me how to use a spear gun, but even though I was not successful that day, Petros speared a nice fish, which we ate for dinner. For the next two days we did nothing but snorkel, until even I learned how to spear a fish. We ate fish both at mid-day and for the evening meal. That was the most enjoyable part of the time I spent in Greece—the best time of my life.

"Oh, I almost forgot. One morning a motor launch appeared at the mouth of our cove and dropped anchor. Five men were on it. They swam off the boat while Petros and I stayed in the house, watching them through the windows. They were Germans; at least Petros said that's the language they were speaking. They weren't there over an hour when a Greek navy patrol boat appeared and pulled alongside. Greek sailors boarded the motor launch to examine the Germans' documents. After a little while, the sailors went back to their own boat and the motor launch pulled up its anchor and left, with the Greek boat following. I don't know why, but that incident bothered Petros, and later that day, when the Bulgarian came again to the house, Petros told him about it. They spoke in Greek, but I could tell what they were talking about because Petros kept pointing to where the motor launch had anchored. Finally the Bulgarian shook his head and in Bulgarian said, 'Don't worry; we know all about it; it's nothing.' I mention that because I was surprised that the Greek patrol boat arrived so soon after the motor launch anchored, and that the Americans seemed to find out about it so quickly. There must have been some observation point near the house, but I never saw it. They seemed to have thought of everything."

For three days Petros and Kolev had done nothing but snorkel and relax, but the next morning the Americans arrived, bringing with them two knapsacks, two canteens and enough canned food and bread for five days. They told Kolev he would be going on a five-day training exercise, similar in distance and difficulty to the mission into Bulgaria. He and Petros were to be dropped off north of Kavalla and proceed northeast to the west side of a town called Xanthi. They gave him the coordinates on the map where he and Petros were to stop and conceal themselves. From there Kolev was to photograph a factory on the west side of Xanthi. They must walk at night, they said, and should arrive before dawn on the third day outside Xanthi, where they were to stay concealed all day. Kolev would take the photographs in the late afternoon, when the sun would be behind him. They explained that he and Petros would have to cross the Nestos River, but that the river had shallow places, and Petros would know where to cross. After sunset on the third day, they were to start their return to a point north of Kavalla, where the Americans would be waiting at dawn on the fifth day. Kolev jotted down map coordinates for that point. They would start that night.

The Americans had given Kolev a small hunting knife that fit on his belt in a sheath, and a watch with a small button on the side that when pushed, illuminated the face. They also gave him two rolls of film, and a very small flashlight for reading the map at night and making entries in his notebook. Petros showed him how to use his jacket to cover his head to hide the light. Kolev noted checkpoints on the map that he should reach to keep on his route, and they told him to log in his notebook the sightings and headings used to find his location en route. Petros would have a weapon, they said. Kolev would not.

"That evening just after dusk, the Americans arrived and we loaded up and drove twenty minutes or so north of Kavalla, where they wished us good luck and departed. I shot my first azimuths, and we began walking on a heading. The night was dark, and I had to stop often to check our location and heading, and to make entries in my notebook. It was slow going because we were climbing steadily. A couple of months earlier, I couldn't have maintained the pace we kept, but I felt good. At midnight, we stopped, opened a can of beans and a small can of sausages, and ate with spoons we had brought from the house. When we finished, Petros told me to use my knife to bury the cans, and he then spread a few leaves and loose dirt where I buried them. Shortly after midnight we began going down, and by morning, at first light, we were approaching a valley where we could see the Nestos River. There we stopped for the day. We hid in scrub bushes and slept until mid-afternoon, but stayed there until dark. We ate again, hid any evidence, and started for the river. At its banks we could see that the water was dark and appeared deep, so we walked north a hundred meters or so until we came to some shallows, and crossed there. Once across I had to orient us again and find new headings, so putting my coat over my head to hide the light, I noted the new headings in my notebook. We started climbing again. The climb that night was very difficult, because the mountains in that area are over fifteen hundred meters high. By midnight we stopped to rest, even though we had stopped often on the way up the mountain. We ate and rested for almost an hour, and I dozed off, but after I had slept about twenty minutes, Petros shook me awake and we started again. In two hours, we had reached the peak and then started going down to the southeast, toward Xanthi, and just before dawn we could see a few lights of the town. At dawn we located the factory, moved into camera range and hid in a tree line above the factory. We were both very tired, and instead of eating, we immediately fell asleep and didn't awaken until early afternoon. Then we ate, I prepared the camera, and about three o'clock started photographing the factory's main building, all the supporting buildings and the cars parked around the buildings. The factory appeared to produce housing material, including bricks, because we saw a kiln behind the main building.

"I took one entire roll of film, and when I finished, we slept again. Petros looked tired. He had circles under his eyes, and the lines in his face seemed deeper. I wondered how a man of his age could endure these long hikes, and the climbing of steep mountains, hour after hour. He was truly a tough man. We woke up at dusk and started back.

"We retraced our route, but we weren't moving as fast as we had on our way there, and because the climbing was difficult, we stopped often. At each stop I would flop on the ground, but Petros would continue standing. He didn't seem to need to rest his body, just to catch his breath."

By the next morning, Kolev remembered, they were approaching the valley of the Nestos River from the east, and at dawn stopped for the day and slept. When it grew dark they went to the river, took off their boots and bathed their feet, and then stuck their heads in the water. The water was cold, and it shocked any remaining clouds of fatigue from their minds. After crossing the river they started the climb to the top of the mountain range north of Kavalla. Climbing most of the night, they began descending toward Kavalla about two in the morning.

"By dawn we still had not reached the point where we were to meet the Americans, so we decided to keep walking in the daylight. About seven we arrived, and the Americans were waiting for us.

"They greeted us warmly and asked how we felt. Petros said we felt fine, but I told them we were exhausted. They all laughed, but I didn't, I was damned tired, and the American agreed with me, saying we looked exhausted, and that I was more honest than Petros. Driving through Kavalla, I enjoyed the smell of coffee and hot bread coming from the little sidewalk cafes lining the narrow streets, and the sight of women throwing buckets of water on the cobble stones in front of their houses and then sweeping them clean with brooms so short they had to bend to use them.

"When we arrived at the house, a nice surprise awaited us. The Greek driver had prepared a small pit with burning charcoal, and over the charcoal were three chickens on a spit that the driver was turning slowly. I could smell the cooking meat when we got out of the jeep. The driver had placed a table and five chairs in the shade under the grape arbor, and on the table were a huge salad and two loaves of bread. A tub sat beside the table, filled with bottles of beer covered with ice. The Bulgarian told Petros and me to pose while he photographed us, and then he took a close-up of our faces. I never saw the photographs before I left on my mission.

"Petros and I decided to go for a quick swim while the chickens were cooking, and when I went into the house to change my clothes, I looked at myself in the bathroom mirror. I was shocked. I looked worse than Petros. Dark circles had formed under my eyes, which were bloodshot. My face was drawn and my cheeks were hollow.

"We felt good after our swim, and sat down to a wonderful meal. The Bulgarian and the American reviewed my notebook and compared my notes with the map while we ate. But they couldn't read some of my notebook entries because writing on the ground, my head covered by my jacket, and using a dim light, some of them were just scribbles. After I helped them with the notes, they said they were very pleased with their accuracy and the headings I had taken and followed. They discussed our exercise with Petros in Greek for quite some time and seemed pleased also by what he told them, because they congratulated me again for my stamina and determination. After we finished eating, the driver cleaned everything up and they left. Petros and I went to bed and slept until the next morning."

Kolev and Petros had done nothing for the next week except swim, snorkel and relax. No one came to the house. At the end of the week the Bulgarian came. He had developed the photographs Kolev had taken of the factory, and they were clear, well focused with sharp imagery. The Bulgarian told Kolev he had done a superb job of adjusting for distance and light. Even Petros patted him on the back.

Markov pushed his chair back, stood and walked around the room, his hands clasped behind his back. "What's interesting about all this," he said, "is that you have such amazing recall of so many details. It's almost as if you are reliving it."

"I do relive it, Mister Markov. I've had eleven years to think of almost nothing else. I've been over that whole experience thousands of times in my mind. I recount every detail over and over, but I'll tell you something, what I've told you so far was child's play compared to what happened later."

Chapter 6

"Three days later the Americans returned, and asked me to sit at the table. Petros went outside. I was ready, they said, and would leave on the mission the next night. Lined up on the table were new clothes, a map of that part of Bulgaria where I was going, a new knapsack, food, new shoes, a Browning pistol, a new notebook, three rolls of film and a Leica camera. Then the briefing began. It lasted the rest of the day."

Markov leaned forward, putting his arms on the desk and moving to the edge of his chair. He stared at Kolev, who paused, glanced at the ceiling, cleared his throat and began counting the fingers of one hand.

"Yeah, that's all they gave me," Kolev said. "Then they spread the map, and the scale was large, one-to-fifty-thousand. I was going near Ribnovo, north of Skrebatno and east of the Mesta River, which as you must know, is the same as the Nestos River in Greece, and runs out of the Rila Mountains—the same river we crossed on my five-day training exercise. The Americans had information that in a cave complex two kilometers south of Ribnovo, just east of the road running from Skrebatno to Ribnovo, medium-range ballistic missiles were being assembled. They said that if they could get coverage of the entrance for a few hours, analysts could make a pretty good guess whether to confirm or reject the information."

The Americans had told Kolev to approach the site from the west and position himself on the east slope of a mountain that ran north and south just opposite the entrance to the cave complex. They showed him that position on the map. From there, he was told to photograph the entrance and all vehicles coming and going, from just after noon until dusk. The position from which he would take the photographs was heavily forested and would conceal him well. It would require two nights to walk there and two nights to return—a five-day mission. He would walk only at night and stay concealed during daylight. They showed him on the map where they would put him across the border, and told him to continue north to the Mesta River. There he had to turn northwest, and proceed to a road leading east out of Gotse Delchev, cross the Mesta River on that road, and immediately get off the road and turn northeast. They warned him to walk just off the crest of a ridgeline going north, paralleling the road from Ognjanovo by Skrebatno to Ribnovo, and never allow himself to be silhouetted on that ridgeline or any other. They told him to verify his position several times a night, and to record his position, the time, the azimuths used to locate his position, and the heading he was following.

"Of course, I had learned all of that during my training. They told me to take the small flashlight we had used during training.

"We then went over the clothing. The shoes were low-tops with rubber soles. Inside the shoes and all the clothing, labels showed they were made in Bulgaria. The knapsack was made in the Soviet Union. The unloaded pistol had no markings; ammunition would be given to me at the border, just before I crossed.

"The camera was the one I had been training with, and they gave me three rolls of film and told me to take two rolls of photographs. The third was a spare in case I lost one. They said not to point the camera at the cave complex until after mid-day, because from where I would be hiding, west of the complex, the morning light could cast reflections off the camera lens and give away my position to the guards outside.

"We then discussed crossing the border. There would be no moon, but three hours later a half moon would appear, and there would be some moonlight the rest of the night. They would take me to within three hundred meters of the border and they told me that when I was ready, to go directly to the fence and cross. 'Don't wait, because the plowed strip will be free of mines there, and the lower strand of the wire will be loosened so that you can crawl under it.' Any footprints left in the plowed strip, they said, would be erased, leaving no trace of my crossing. I would have to walk hard for one hour after crossing to clear the immediate border area, staying out of valleys and just below ridgelines.

"Didn't they show you on the map exactly where you should walk?" Markov interrupted, as he made an entry in his notepad.

"No," Kolev answered. "That would have been impossible. They showed me where I had to go, but how I got there was up to me. They didn't know what kinds of things I might run into that might have forced me to change my route." Kolev took a cigarette, lit it, and blew a stream of smoke toward the ceiling.

"Then they talked about my return, saying I had to come to the same point where I crossed and stop at least one hundred meters inside Bulgaria. They told me to be there before dawn on the morning of the fifth day after my crossing, in time to cross the border while it was still dark. First light would be at 0542 hours that morning. When I got to the right place to cross, they told me to point my flashlight across the border and turn it on and off twice, in rapid succession. At a heading of one hundred and eighty-four degrees, about three kilometers south of the border, I would see the lights of a vehicle turn on, and stay on for thirty seconds. I should not attempt to cross until I saw that signal. Again, the lower strand of fence wire would be loosened. If they did not see my signal on the morning I was supposed to arrive, they would wait for me and be prepared to signal me for four more nights. If they saw no signal by that time, they would assume something happened to me and leave. I asked how they would see my small flashlight signal from three kilometers away, and they said some people would be waiting for me just across the border, and they would see my signal. When it was safe for me to cross, those people would radio the vehicle to give the signal.

"They told me to get a good night's sleep, and they would return in the morning.

"I didn't get a good night's sleep. Petros and I had a quiet dinner, and neither of us said very much. Petros knew I was leaving the next day. We went to bed early, but I couldn't fall asleep. I thought about my life since deciding to escape from Bulgaria. I had wanted only to go somewhere to find a good job, and to be able to live a better life than I could in Bulgaria. But there I was, a trained espionage agent, about to enter Bulgaria clandestinely as an agent of a nation considered an enemy by the Bulgarian government. I was excited to think that perhaps when I returned, my government might treat me as a hero, maybe even make me a member of the Bulgarian Intelligence Service.

"The Americans seemed to have an interesting job in Greece, but then again, the life of a member of an intelligence service might be dangerous. And I admit, I was scared. Even though I intended to turn myself in, someone could shoot me at the border, or perhaps the Americans and the Greeks didn't know as much about the border and the border guards as they thought they did. What if some border guard shot me before giving me a chance to explain what I was doing there?

"In the middle of the night I got up and walked outside and sat under the grape arbor, looking at the cove. There was a half moon, and the light was shining on the water—like thousands of fireflies. That would have been a nice place to live."

Kolev paused in his story and smiled, nodding his head slightly. He took out a handkerchief and blew his nose, and to Markov, it was obvious that Kolev remembered that house, and that time, with nostalgia.

"Then I heard a click, and turned to see Petros lighting a cigarette. He gave it to me, and lit one for himself, and said, 'The thinking about such things is always worse than the doing of them. You are about to commit an act against Communism, and I have suffered much because of Communists. I know God will be on your side.' Then he went back to bed.

"I knew I would never see Petros again after tomorrow. I would miss him, and I wished I could have him as a friend for life. He didn't talk much, but when he spoke his words were worth listening to, and it was comforting just to be in his presence. I liked him a lot and hoped that God, if there was one, would be on his side too."

Kolev said he awakened several hours later, still sitting in the chair. Since there was only a hint of light in the east, he went to bed and fell asleep again. At nine in the morning, Petros shook him awake. The Americans were already there. After he had washed and dressed, Petros fixed a big breakfast for them, and there was much light conversation. Nothing was said about the mission.

"When I finished eating, the Bulgarian opened a bag he had placed on the counter in the kitchen, and took from it a dried sausage, bread, fruit, and six flat round discs that he explained were high-energy concentrated chocolate patties from American army field rations. Packing these in the knapsack, he added three small cans of beans, two packages of dried fruit and a half roll of toilet paper. He gave me a plastic bag to protect the camera, and a smaller plastic bag for the notebook.

"Again we went over the mission route and reviewed the functions and settings for the camera. They asked if I had any questions, and when I said, no, they asked me what I would do if I got caught. That stumped me. My plans were to turn myself in, so that wasn't one of my worries. But, right away, before I could answer, they said, 'If you are caught, tell them every thing you know, as quickly as possible.'"

"Why do you think they told you that?" Markov asked, surprised.'"

"Well, they explained that if I got caught, there would be no question in the minds of the interrogators what I was doing in Bulgaria. There would be a hostile and brutal interrogation, and if I tried to withhold information, they would beat it out of me. The American said they didn't want me to suffer that, and for that reason, to protect themselves and me, they had taken particular care not to let me learn anything that would be damaging to them, even if I told everything. After that conversation, they told me to relax the rest of the day, to nap if possible. They would be back for me late in the afternoon.

"Needless to say, I didn't nap, and Petros didn't want me to swim. He said I should conserve my strength because, as I had learned on our five-day training exercise, my mission would be strenuous.

"When it became obvious that I wasn't going to sleep, Petros told me a horrible story. He had never talked so much during the months we had been together. He said that during the occupation of Greece by the Germans and Bulgarians during the world war, he belonged to a guerrilla unit of some two hundred men. They operated in the area where we had been training. Early one morning, far west of there, his unit had attacked a German truck convoy and killed many Germans, leaving at least a dozen trucks burning. About eighty guerillas had taken part in the attack, and they began withdrawing, trying to make their way east and eventually north to higher mountains where they could regroup and stay hidden for several weeks. Their leader, 'the *Kapitanios*' Petros called him, was a tough, hard man, and a great leader, who happened to have his wife and infant son with him when the attack was made. He had been moving them to a village further north, where the inhabitants were totally loyal to him. After the attack, the Germans moved dozens of infantry units into the area to track and destroy the band, and the band stayed on the move for four days. The mother of the *Kapitanios'* son walked with them, often feeding the infant from her breasts as they walked. They eventually reached some high mountains, very rough terrain, where it was virtually impossible for large infantry units to operate, and concealed themselves in caves and waited for the Germans to give up the search. Two days later the Germans approached the area. The Greeks could see them in the valley below. Several German patrols came near to where the band was hiding, and the *Kapitanios'* baby began to cry. The mother tried desperately to stop the baby from crying, but when it became obvious the baby couldn't be silenced, the *Kapitanios* took his knife and cut the infant's throat. It was his only child at the time. He did that, Petros said, because the infant would have revealed their position to the Germans, and the *Kapitanios* had to save his fighters.

"'I tell you this story for one reason,' Petros said. 'If during your mission, you reach a point where you believe you are too exhausted to go on, or the risks are so great you can't face them, I want you to remember one thing; the West you wish to go to for sanctuary and a better life, exists because of men who came before you, men who made great sacrifices for causes they believed in. You are now being given a chance to make your contribution. Cherish it!'

Kolev shook his head as if puzzled, and after a long pause, said, "That story has haunted me through the years, and I wondered what kind of man could kill his own child, but I knew Petros was that kind of man. I could never be like him."

The Americans had come late that day. It was time to go. Kolev remembered that they had helped him arrange his knapsack, the heavy things on the bottom, and the other things he would be carrying. The American wore a sweater and a jacket, and Kolev had noticed that he was wearing a pistol in a shoulder holster under his jacket. He took the pistol Kolev would be carrying, put a round in the chamber, inserted a full magazine in the grip, and put the pistol in his own belt. He gave Kolev a spare loaded magazine to carry in a pocket.

When they started for the jeep, Petros embraced Kolev, patted him on the cheek and winked. They shook hands, and Petros said, "I'll be here when you return. God bless you."

The American had put Kolev in the back seat and climbed in beside the Bulgarian, who was driving. They drove through Kavalla, then Drama, and north into the mountains. Soon there were no more paved roads, and they followed dirt paths until they ended, then drove through rough terrain. Later they came upon a Greek army truck with soldiers in the back, and stopped behind it. From the front of the truck, a Greek officer appeared, and as he headed for the jeep, the American and the Bulgarian got out to talk with him.

"After a few minutes the Bulgarian and the American got back in the jeep, and we started forward very slowly, following the truck. Neither vehicle used lights. After a half-hour or so we stopped, and the soldiers got out of the truck and went forward on foot. The officer stayed with us. The American told me that in about one hour we would leave the truck, and go forward in the jeep for approximately another half-kilometer, where I would get out of the jeep and go to the border and cross. My heart was pounding. He said that about one hundred meters from the border, the Greek soldiers would be spread out to cover me in case something happened, so if I heard a noise as I approached the border, I shouldn't be frightened. While we waited, the Greek officer spoke into a hand-held radio from time to time.

"Soon we were told by the Greek officer to start. The officer got in the back seat of the jeep with me, and we moved forward very slowly. When we stopped, we all got out of the jeep. The American told me to sight my compass directly north and to follow the needle to the border. He handed me the pistol, which I stuck in my belt. We all shook hands, and in whispers they wished me good luck. They assured me they would be there waiting for me when I returned.

"I sighted the compass directly north and began walking slowly, following the needle. It was very dark, and I'd walked perhaps two hundred meters, when I saw the dim outline of the fence. Someone coughed to my right. A Greek soldier. I crouched, and ran toward the fence.

Chapter 7

"I got to within twenty meters of the fence, dropped and crawled to it on my stomach. The lowest strand of the wire was very loose, so I took my knapsack off and pushed it under the fence, and then crawled under it, stood, grabbed my knapsack and sprinted up a gradual incline. Actually, I didn't sprint—I ran like hell! I stopped about a hundred meters beyond the fence. My mouth was dry, my heart thumped, and my legs shook. I didn't hear a sound. The area was heavily wooded, so when I calmed down I began walking farther up the slope, and after about two hundred meters, stopped again. I decided to turn west and walk parallel to the border until I came to a border post, so I walked down an incline and crossed a shallow valley, then walked up another incline and came to a stretch of flat terrain. Continuing on that for fifteen or twenty minutes, I came to a place where the ground began to slope away again, and decided to stop there and wait for the moon to appear. A couple of hours later, as the Americans said it would, a half-moon began to rise, and as soon as I could see better, I started down the slope and was soon in another heavily wooded area.

"Off to my left I heard the sound of a vehicle engine, and then saw headlights that stayed on a few seconds, and then went off. I heard a vehicle door slam shut and voices, so I started walking in that direction. In a few minutes I came to a clearing, and where a low one-story building stood with two trucks and a jeep parked in front. Lights showed inside the building, so I walked into the clearing and shouted, asking if anyone was inside. The door opened, spreading light into the clearing, so I stepped into the light with my hands up, and I shouted again, asking if I could come inside. Sounds of scuffling and excited voices came from inside. Three soldiers ran from the building carrying rifles, shouting at me to put my hands up. They were already up. I stood still and waited until they reached me. Two of them approached slowly, pointing their rifles at me, and the third pointed a light at my face and asked what I was doing there. I told him I'd been sent from Greece and wished to speak to an officer. By this time there were six or eight more soldiers coming toward me, all armed with rifles. They crowded around, and the guy with the light shouted, 'what's your name, and what're you doin' here?' But before I could answer, he said, 'Come with us!'

"Inside there was a large ante-room, where it appeared the soldiers lounged when they weren't on patrol, and they pushed me into the middle of the room. A door opened on the left and a senior lieutenant came out. He looked me up and down and ordered, 'Search him!' They took my knapsack and put it on a desk, ran their hands over me and found the pistol. One of the soldiers removed the magazine, ejected the round from the chamber and put it on the desk. They went through my pockets and took the extra magazine and the rolls of film then emptied my knapsack and took the camera from the plastic bag."

Markov pushed his chair back and stood. Placing his hands on his hips, he walked around the room for a few moments. Kolev stopped talking and watched him closely. Markov bent over, stretching from the waist, returned to his chair and sat. "By God," he said, "you did what you intended to do, but it's unbelievable how you, a tractor mechanic from a collective farm, ended up at that border post. It's a helluva story—how peoples' lives can get so screwed up—but please go on."

"Okay, well, you're right, I can't believe it myself. Anyway, the officer asked, 'Who are you, and what are you doing here?'

"'My name is Ivan Kolev and I've been sent on an espionage mission by the Americans,' I answered. 'But I was forced to do this, and came here to turn myself in. I am a loyal Bulgarian.'

"'What's your mission?' he demanded, 'and were you sent to kill anyone?'

"'No, sir,' I said. 'My mission is to photograph a site near Ribnovo.'

"'Then why do you have this pistol?'

"'They gave it to me to protect myself while on this mission,' I answered.

"The officer motioned for me to sit down, ordered all the soldiers, except a sergeant, out of the room, and sat behind the desk. The sergeant sat too, and prepared to take notes.

"'Have you been sent to contact anyone in Bulgaria?' he asked.

"'No sir,' I said. 'Only to take photographs and nothing more.'

"The officer then called two soldiers and told them to lock me in the next room. In that small room with only a cot, the soldiers told me to take off my shoes and belt, and when I did so, they left and locked the door. It was two o'clock in the morning.

"I sat on the cot for a long while, but eventually lay down and slept. At six in the morning I awoke when the door opened, and a soldier brought me a bowl of lentils and a glass of water on a tray. After eating, I knocked on the door and asked the guard if I could go to the bathroom. He said, 'Wait,' and closed the door. But in a few minutes two soldiers came with my shoes, told me to put them on, and then led me out the back to another building that had toilets and showers. When we went back to the room, they took my shoes again, locked the door, and in a few minutes I fell right to sleep.

"At nine o'clock the door opened again and a colonel entered, with a soldier behind him carrying a chair. I jumped to attention, but the colonel said, 'Sit down, son,' and he pulled the chair close to the cot and sat. The soldier left.

"'I have come from Sofia,' he said, 'and I'm going to take you there where we can talk more comfortably, but first tell me a bit about yourself, and why you're here.'

"I told him my name, and the same things I told the lieutenant the night before.

"'How much time do you have before you are supposed to be back in Greece?' he asked.

"I was put across the border last night, I said, and am to be back at the place where I crossed before dawn of the fifth morning from today. But sir, I continued, I don't intend to go back, I'm a loyal Bulgarian and was forced to come on this mission for the Americans, and I came here only with the intention of turning myself in, so I could tell you everything.

"'Good lad!' he said. 'But tell me, how did you, such a loyal Bulgarian, find yourself in Greece, being forced to come here on an espionage mission for the Americans?'

"Well, it is a long story, sir, but I'll tell you all about it.

"'Good,' he said, patting me on the knee, 'let's go to Sofia and then you tell me.'" He got up and left the room.

In a few minutes a soldier entered with Kolev's shoes and belt. Kolev put them on and was led out to the front of the building, where the colonel was waiting with a driver and a jeep. They put Kolev in the back seat, and his knapsack, camera and pistol were in the front seat next to the colonel. They started for Sofia.

Kolev remembered that the drive to Sofia took about three hours, and during the drive the colonel asked Kolev about his background, where he came from, what his parents did, where he had worked, and how much education he had.

"He was very polite, and paid close attention to everything I said. We got to Sofia, and drove to a large building that could have been on the south side of the city, I wasn't sure where we were, because you can't see very well from the back seat of a jeep, and I don't know Sofia that well anyway. We stopped in front of two large, arched wooden doors, where the driver blew the horn. A panel opened from inside and someone peered out. Immediately the doors swung open, and we drove through to a courtyard. When we got out of the jeep I saw two armed guards standing at the entrance doors and another guard at the entrance to the building."

"Was this building the Central Prison?" Markov asked.

"No. I don't know what it was, but inside there were cells, and little rooms that I think were interrogation rooms. We went into a large reception room, where a sergeant sat behind a desk. He jumped to attention, as did two other soldiers sitting in chairs against the wall."

The colonel had told the sergeant to put Kolev in a cell, and had left. The two soldiers escorted Kolev down a long dark hall, to a small room with a table and pale green walls. They told him to take off all his clothes and put them on the table. When he did, they took him to a shower room next door, and watched while he showered and dried off with a towel they handed him, and then led him back to the room where he had undressed. His clothes were gone, but on the table were a gray, one-piece jumpsuit and a pair of rubber sandals, and when he was dressed they led him to a cell and locked him in. The cell contained a cot and one chair, but no window. Kolev stretched out on the cot, and within a few minutes was asleep.

"I don't know how long I'd slept when the cell door opened and the colonel entered, sat on the chair facing me and told me to sit on the bunk. 'Mister Ivan Kolev,' he said, 'I've had the opportunity to learn something about you since I left you, and you have a clean working man's record, an uncle in the Communist Party, and parents who are decent and hard working, serving the people on a productive collective farm. I don't understand how you got yourself in the position you now find yourself, but I'm here to help you clear all this up. I presume you left Bulgaria illegally, is that correct?'

Kolev said he nodded.

"Then tell me why and how you left Bulgaria."

Kolev said he told the colonel everything he could think of about his past: his service in the army, work on the collective, and why he was unhappy there, the reason he went to Sofia and why, after he was unable to find a job, had decided to escape to Greece. He told him of his chance meeting with the former border guard, and what he had learned that led him to believe he could cross the border without being caught. He told the colonel how he had traveled to the border area, walked to the border, and hid from the border guards, and how he had crossed the fence and walked into a Greek ambush.

"He asked me about my interrogation by the Greek in great detail, and when I described the Greek interrogator, the colonel said, 'Ah, yes, Mitsos; he has been there many years, and does a good job. But he's a mean bastard.'

"I also, of course, told him about my meeting with the Americans and how, after they had finished questioning me, they told me that I couldn't migrate to the West as the Greek interrogator had promised, but first must go on an espionage mission for them. I told him about feeling tricked, when my only goal had been to go somewhere to find a good job.

"'We shall talk more about the Americans,' he said, 'but first tell me what your mission is.' I told him about being instructed to go to the area of Ribnovo and photograph the cave complex where the Americans said missiles were being assembled. He questioned me about where I had to go to take the photographs, and what route they had told me to take to leave the area afterwards. Oh, he also asked me lots of questions about my mission I couldn't answer."

"Why, what questions couldn't you answer about your mission?" Markov asked.

"Well, I couldn't answer how the Americans knew that missiles were being assembled in the cave complex, or why the Americans didn't try to have one of their agents in Bulgaria take the photographs. Things like that."

"Go on."

"Then he questioned me about the Americans, and asked for physical descriptions. I described. them as best I could, and he seemed pleased that I had observed so much. He wasn't surprised that they never used a name in front of me. When I repeated several times that they never used names, he said, 'I believe you, son. Those men aren't amateurs. They don't make such mistakes.'"

Kolev recounted that the colonel left the cell, but about an hour later returned with maps of southern Bulgaria and northern Greece. Kolev showed him his route of escape. He was still uncertain where he crossed the border into Greece, but could show in detail where Petros and he had conducted the training hikes.

They had spent the rest of the day discussing Kolev's training. The colonel asked Kolev to identify on the map the location of the house he had lived in, but he was vague about the exact location, because there were numerous coves on the coast south of Kavalla, and several had small rock formations. Kolev told him he thought the area was closely watched, and described how quickly the Greeks responded when the German boat anchored at the mouth of the cove. The colonel wanted to know which of the Americans had taught him to work with a map and compass, and which had taught him to use a weapon, which one devised his training schedule and took the lead in briefing him about his mission. They talked for several hours.

"He asked me many questions about the Bulgarian who worked for the Americans, especially what he looked like, and any special marks I had noticed on his face or hands. That question reminded me that the Bulgarian had an L-shaped scar on his chin. The colonel said, 'Good, we'll get back to him.'

"When the colonel left, an evening meal and a pack of cigarettes were sent in. I slept not long after eating, but about midnight I heard the sounds of someone being beaten. I could hear muffled, harsh voices, the sounds of the beating, and a man's screams. It seemed to go on for hours, and I was so afraid that might happen to me that I couldn't sleep."

In the morning, shortly after they brought Kolev a morning meal, the colonel had returned. He sat close to Kolev and began speaking in a soft, almost fatherly manner, saying, 'Son, you shouldn't be here. You broke our country's laws by escaping from the country illegally. We issue visas for legal departures, and you are a candidate for a long prison sentence, but I don't want you to go to prison. You strike me as a polite young man who has no political agenda and no ideological instincts that would drive you to undertake activities against the people, against the state. But here you sit,' he said, 'an illegal escapee in Bulgaria on an espionage mission for a hostile government. Your reason for escaping is not acceptable; every citizen can find employment here. And your reason for accepting an espionage mission is questionable. Some people would send you to trial and demand the death penalty without a second thought. Do you understand that?' he asked.

"I said, 'Yes sir, but you know I came here on this mission with the intention of helping Bulgaria, not to do harm.'

"The colonel looked at me for long moments, and said, 'Ivan, do you honestly think that you could stand before a court, explain to the judges that you escaped illegally, are in Bulgaria as a foreign agent, and that the judges would thank you for having done a great service for the Peoples Republic of Bulgaria? What I think is not relevant.'

"I didn't know what to say. I began to cry, and asked the colonel for help, saying I didn't want to be put in prison, or be executed. Without a word the colonel got up and left the room.

"That was probably the worst moment of my life. At least up to that point. I felt helpless, with no way out, and was drained—totally."

Within an hour, he said, the colonel had returned with another officer, a captain, and a soldier who brought a chair for the captain. The colonel said, "I want you to work with this officer, describe to him the features of the Bulgarian who works for the Americans. The captain will draw those features on a pad."

Kolev said he began to describe the Bulgarian, with the captain asking about his hairline and forehead, his eyes and nose, his lips and chin and the shape of his face. The captain was a capable artist. He got the eyes right, had difficulty with the lips and chin, but after many changes he made a remarkably close likeness of the Bulgarian. Kolev was amazed at how much the drawing looked like the Bulgarian. When they finished, the colonel thanked the captain, and the captain took his drawing pad and chair and left.

"After the captain departed, the colonel moved his chair a few meters from me, and when he spoke, his tone was not as fatherly. He said, 'Ivan, I believe I can save your life, and I will speak to you as a man, because what we are about to discuss is not a matter for an errant boy. I have great sympathy for you, and believe you meant no harm, and that you are a victim of your own bad judgement. So I'm prepared to testify at a trial that you should be punished for escaping illegally, but that you deserve leniency, because you, young, immature and naive, accepted an espionage mission on behalf of a foreign government because you were coerced, and that you turned yourself in. If I am persuasive, you will be sent to prison, but with a reduced sentence. I can't promise, but I'll try.'

"'Colonel,' I said, 'I'll do whatever you want.'"

"'I'm not finished,' the colonel said, raising a hand. 'There may be another option for you,' he continued. 'The Americans, and the Greeks, have been sending agents into Bulgaria on espionage missions for years. Many we have caught and executed, but you are the first to turn himself in, and we need someone loyal to us inside their cross-border espionage operation. I can help you accomplish your mission for the Americans, and help you return to Greece. Since you will have completed a mission for them, there's a good chance they'll trust you more than the last time you were in their hands, and if you tell them you are willing to undertake more missions for them, you'll learn more about their activities. You must ask them to pay you so much a month, and to give you a bonus each time you complete a mission. You'll tell them that once you've earned enough money to provide for a comfortable start for yourself in the West, you'll expect them to help you resettle. We presume they'll send you on future missions. Each time they do, we'll meet you so you can report to us what you've learned, and once we're satisfied that you've learned all you're going to, we'll tell you to inform them that you don't want to go on any more missions, and want to be resettled in America. Once you arrive in America, or wherever you are established in the West, you'll communicate clandestinely with us. We'll then contact you, and you can continue working for us. We'll help you in the West, both with advice and guidance about how to improve your success there, and with funds to make your life easier.'

"'But how would I communicate with you?' I asked."

"'From wherever you are you will merely address a postcard to your mother at the collective farm, and tell your mother where you are and your address, that you are doing well and that you like your new job. Something like that. Nothing will be important but your mother's address and your address. Your mother won't receive the postcard because we'll intercept it, and then contact you. Whoever contacts you will tell you that he has a message from your mother, and that your uncle Khristo is well. When he tells you that, you'll know I sent him. Now, I'm going to leave. You think about this. If you agree, you'll be entering the life of a clandestine agent for your government, and it could be dangerous, but you'll be considered a hero in your country for the rest of your life. And if you're smart, and follow our instructions, you'll be all right. I'll return in the morning for your decision, and if your answer is yes, we'll depart immediately to prepare you for your return to Greece.'

"With that, he stood to leave, and for the first time, he shook my hand."

Markov leaned back, folding his hands in his lap. He stared at the desk for a few moments and said, "Incredible. That colonel threatened you with prison, and then recruited you as an agent to save you, and I'll bet he knew all along what he was going to do. At that point he made you—what do they call it—a double agent."

"Yeah, I guess so," Kolev said. "Yep, you're right, he did."

"Tell me about the colonel," Markov asked.

Kolev pushed his chair back and stood. He raised his right hand several inches above his head, and said, "He was tall, about up to here, taller than I am." He spread both hands in front of his abdomen. "He was big around the middle, and when his shirt was buttoned there was a little role of fat at the top of his collar. His hair was closely cropped and turning white, especially at the sides." Sitting, Kolev said, "But he had soft blue eyes, and a pleasant smile, and he was always polite—that is, until later."

"Okay, please go on," Markov said, making notes.

"Why?" Kolev asked, "You gonna try to find him?"

"How could we?" Markov asked. "You don't even know his name, do you?"

"No, I don't know his name," Kolev said.

"Okay, then please go on."

"All right, well, I slept little that night, although within an hour after the colonel left, I knew I had to accept his offer. To turn it down meant at least a long prison term for me. When I returned to Greece, with the colonel's help, the Americans would believe that I had faithfully performed a mission for them, and if they sent me back to Bulgaria on another mission, I could, with little risk, turn myself in again. And, it seemed to me that I could control the number of these missions simply by telling the Americans at a certain point that I had served them long enough, and wanted to be resettled. Whether I re-contacted the Bulgarian service after being resettled in the West would be up to me.

"I guess it was sometime after midnight when I fell asleep. The next day would be a long one."

Chapter 8

▼

Kolev said he had awakened before dawn and was momentarily confused, unsure where he was. His eyes focused on a guard who had entered his cell and was silhouetted by the light hanging from the ceiling. The guard ordered him up, escorted him to the bathroom, and when he returned to his cell, the guard said a meal would be brought to him shortly, then left. Within a few minutes another guard entered, bringing a tray with dishes of sausages, fried cheese, a bowl of yogurt, slices of onion, black bread and a pitcher of cold water. Kolev inhaled the aroma and smiled. He was home.

"I had just lain back on the cot to smoke a cigarette when the colonel entered my cell. I started to stand, but the colonel put his hand on my shoulder to keep me from rising. Standing over me, he asked for my decision. I said, 'Colonel I want to serve Bulgaria, and prove my loyalty, to work for you against the Americans.'

"The colonel patted me on the cheek, and said, 'My boy, you're doing the right thing. Your fatherland and your people come before everything.'"

He said the colonel pulled the chair close to his bunk and sat. In a slow and deliberate manner he explained how he would prepare Kolev for his return to Greece. They would leave immediately in a jeep with a driver to the area just north of where Kolev had crossed the border and then drive the route the Americans had given him to approach the place where he was to take the photographs. The colonel said he would help take the photographs, assist Kolev to prepare his notes, and return him to the border to be put across safely at the time the Americans had planned.

"Dawn was just breaking when we left the prison gates, heading south. North of the Greek border we turned east, and driving over rough terrain arrived in mid-afternoon about two kilometers north of the point where I had crossed the border.

"Once there, the colonel had me shoot an azimuth at the highest of two mountain peaks north of us and record the compass reading. From a dirt road running along a ridgeline we took compass readings at various points as we proceeded to the Mesta River. There we got out of the jeep and walked for about an hour along the west side of the river, heading northwest toward Gotse Delchev. We spent the night on a hill a few kilometers south of Gotse Delchev. The driver built a fire and took three bayonets from the jeep. We speared bread and sausages on the bayonets and heated them over the fire. We also shared a bottle of wine.

"Before we slept—in sleeping bags that had been packed in the jeep—the colonel told me the Americans would debrief me in detail about the route I had traveled. But, he said, in the morning, using a map, he would work out compass readings to various terrain features on my route, because we would not have time to walk the entire route, or drive the jeep to many of the areas where I would have walked had I carried out the mission by myself.

"The colonel and I sat up rather late, talking by the fire. The colonel gazed at the dark silhouettes of the mountain peaks around us and remarked how beautiful our country was. 'But,' he said, 'our people have a long history of oppression, misery and poverty.' He talked about the five hundred years of Ottoman occupation, and then said, 'We endured the reign of the foreign King Ferdinand, and his rule was more harsh than that of the Turks. Our people were decimated and starved by the Balkan Wars, and the first Great War. Then we had Boris as king, the son of Ferdinand, and still the people had nothing. People were executed on a whim. The monarchy and its supporters had everything, and the people were left the crumbs. Communists were persecuted, because the Communist Party had fought underground against these ruling parties for decades before we took over at the end of the second Great War, thanks to the Russians. My own father had been a Communist activist since long before I was born.

"'But I became a Communist,' he said, 'one day in September, when I was eight years old. On the morning of that day, three truckloads of royalist soldiers arrived in my village, ordering everyone from their homes. A major read out the names of eighteen men—I said men, but two of them were seventeen—and they read my father's name. They lined those men up against a stone wall of a pen where we kept sheep. All the women and we children were standing off a ways, crying and begging, but the soldiers paid no attention. The major stepped in front of the first man; an old man named Stoyanov, pulled his pistol, cocked it and shot Stoyanov in the forehead. A terrible mess blew from his head, and his body was knocked against the wall before it fell and lay quivering on the ground. With that, one of the young men fell to his knees and began begging for his life, but a soldier walked over and struck him in the face with his rifle butt, and when the man fell backwards, the soldier plunged his bayonet into his chest. The man's wife ran screaming to him, but another soldier caught her by the hair, jerked her around, slashed her across the breasts with a knife, and then dragged her by the hair back to where the women and children were standing. She bled terribly, but she survived. Her husband took a long time to die. The major motioned to the next man, who had been standing next to Stoyanov, and the soldiers put a rope around his neck and dragged him to a tree a few meters away. They threw the end of the rope over a limb and four of them hoisted the man about two meters off the ground. His hands had not been tied, so he grasped the rope, trying to keep it from choking him, but soon his strength gave out, and he died there, kicking at the end of that rope. My father shouted something about long live the Communist Party, and the major went over to him and shot him in the mouth. When he fell backward the major shot him in the chest. One by one they shot the remaining men, and then they got in their trucks and left. No authorities ever came to our village to help, and people from the nearby villages were afraid to help us. Once you see that sort of thing son, you'll never forget, and you'll fight them the rest of your life.'"

Kolev paused, placed an elbow on the desk and rested his chin on his hand. For a moment he seemed to lose his train of thought.

"Go on, what did the colonel say next?" Markov asked.

Kolev stared intently at Markov, and said, as if there had been no interruption:

"The colonel spoke in low tones, and very emotionally, and I felt at the time that he was pouring his heart out to me. Later, I've thought often that he may also have been trying to ensure that I had some ideological reason and enough patriotism to do what he had asked me to do. I'm still not sure, but he did open my eyes. There was a reason the Communist Party had come to power in Bulgaria, and perhaps I had stupid, selfish reasons for wanting to escape from my own country. Our history, as the colonel presented it, and the suffering of our people, made my actions appear unimportant. Right then I vowed to myself to do my very best for him."

The next morning the driver had awakened early, made coffee, then woke the colonel and Kolev, and served them bread and fresh fruit. Then they drove to the west side of Gotse Delchev, crossed the Mesta River and turned north on a dirt path until it ended. There they stopped. The colonel spread a map out on the hood of the jeep and in great detail went through the route Kolev would have taken if he had walked to that place. The map was a large-scale military map, with more detail than the map Kolev had trained with. The colonel chose a number of terrain features on Kolev's supposed route, worked out compass readings from points on the route to those features, and then had Kolev note those headings in his notebook, and what his location would have been had he actually shot the compass readings. When they finished, they walked north along the east side of the ridgeline that would take them to a position opposite the place where he would take the photographs.

"We arrived there about mid-afternoon and had a clear view of the target. The sun was behind me, as the Americans told me it must be for me to take good photographs."

Kolev stood, put both hands on top of his head, and said excitedly, "But you wouldn't believe what was in front of the target I was supposed to photograph. Perhaps a hundred military vehicles were lined up on the road in front of the target: trucks and tank carriers loaded with tanks, and road-clearing equipment. The column extended over a kilometer on either side of the target.

Sitting again, he said, "Look, I told the colonel, they are blocking the view."

"The colonel grinned, and said, 'Yes. They've been there since early this morning and they'll be there for two more days. See, the soldiers are camping on the side of the road. It has all the appearances of an armored column being moved, and the American satellites will certainly notice them, too. Now, you go ahead and take the photographs as you were instructed.'

"I spent a little over an hour taking photographs, shooting two rolls of film. None of the vehicles moved, and there was no other traffic on the road. I took many photographs of the soldiers in the area, and while we were there, the colonel had me take several compass readings to obvious terrain features and record them.

"We left in late afternoon, walked back to the jeep and drove toward Gotse Delchev and turned south. I dozed off in the back of the jeep. When I awoke we were on a dirt road, which the colonel said was used to supply the border posts in that area. The driver stopped and pulled the jeep off the road, driving slowly up an incline through some trees until we came to a small clearing. The colonel told me that we were about three kilometers north of the point where I was to cross the border to return to Greece."

With the map again spread out on the hood of the jeep, the colonel had worked out the route Kolev would have taken had he returned to that point on foot. He chose more terrain features and worked out compass readings to them from points along Kolev's route, and did the same for the points on the route from where Kolev would have taken the compass readings. He made Kolev record all this information in his notebook to prove to the Americans that he had been to those areas. Darkness fell before they finished, but the driver brought a lantern from the jeep and they continued.

When they had finished with the map and compass recordings, the colonel briefed Kolev on what to do when he next crossed the border on a mission for the Americans. He wrote down a telephone number and made Kolev memorize it. He said when Kolev next crossed he should immediately turn himself in to the nearest border guard post, and tell the officer on duty, and only the officer, to telephone the number and say to the person who answers, "Tell Hakim the oak tree has fallen." He said that message would alert the duty officer receiving the call who would have standing instructions to notify the colonel and to order the border guard officer to keep Kolev comfortable and safe. The colonel said Kolev would be picked up in a matter of hours and taken to Sofia.

"Then the colonel ordered me to walk in and out of a briar patch. The briars put little tears in my clothing and scratched my hands. He then made me roll on the ground several times until my clothes were soiled and then rub dirt on my hands and wipe it off on my clothing. While I did that, the driver prepared a light meal, and as we ate the colonel had me take off my shoes, gave them to the driver, and instructed him to rub the soles on a large rock nearby, to make them look worn. He took almost everything out of my knapsack, those things that I would have consumed during the mission.

"For the rest of the time we spent together he talked to me about how I should behave back in Greece, saying that I probably would be put back in the house by the sea with Petros. He told me to ask Petros to help me learn Greek. It would be valuable, he said, if I could learn enough Greek to be able to understand what the Americans and Petros said to each other. He told me to ingratiate myself with the Americans, to praise everything American, and ask the Americans to help me learn English so I could read about the history of America.

"He said, 'Tell the Americans that it is the dream of every Bulgarian to go to America. Thank them frequently for the chance they have given you to work for them. Be very attentive to any slips they might make in the use of their names, and remember everything said about their families or where they came from. Ask the Bulgarian where he is from, and find out what you can about him. Perhaps he has family here. If so, we can use them to get to him.'

"It was shortly after midnight when the colonel said it was time for me to go, that it would take me about three hours to reach the point where I must cross the border. He gave me a compass reading and told me to follow it to the border. He said all border guards had been instructed to stay away from that area until dawn. He shook my hand and gave me a warm embrace. I turned to walk toward the border, but after a few steps, I stopped and turned back to him, and said, 'Colonel I wish to thank you for the chance you have given me to serve my country, and for helping me as you have. I shall be indebted to you forever.' The colonel smiled, and said, 'Go, boy, we shall meet again.' I turned and started walking."

It had been a cloudy night, but after Kolev walked a short distance, his eyes became accustomed to the dark, so he had no trouble finding his way. He stopped frequently and took compass readings to make sure his course was true.

"After almost three hours of walking, I saw the fence about one hundred meters in front of me, and there I sat and listened for a few minutes. The only sound was the barking of a dog in the distance. The sound was from the south, probably from some Greek village. I saw no lights.

"Let me stop you for a minute."

"Yes, Mister Markov."

"At that point in your life you had escaped illegally from Bulgaria to Greece and you had been recruited by the Americans to return to Bulgaria on an espionage mission. You turned yourself in, then accepted recruitment by the Bulgarian Intelligence Service to return to Greece and the Americans as a double agent."

"Well, yes, except I wasn't really recruited by the Americans. I just pretended to be."

"I know, I know, but what I want to ask is, what was the state of your mind then, when you were preparing to cross back into Greece? You knew that if you were caught as a Bulgarian agent in Greece you could be executed."

"Yeah, you're right. Thinking back, I was quite calm, and totally confident that to behave around the Americans as the colonel had told me would be easy. I knew of nothing that would make the Americans suspect me; I went on the mission as they asked, and it was not my fault I couldn't take the photographs of the target site. I had photographs to prove that there were military vehicles blocking my view, and I knew I had the backing of the colonel and my government. No, I felt very confident."

Interesting. Please go on."

"Well, as the Americans instructed me, I took a compass reading of one hundred eighty-four degrees, then turned my flashlight on and off twice quickly. Within a few seconds I saw the lights of a car flash on and stay lit for approximately thirty seconds. The lights were a long distance from the border. That was my signal to cross, if you recall.

"I waited a bit, to make sure there were no sounds around me, then stood and sprinted toward the fence. As they had promised, the bottom wire was loose, and I crawled under it, pushing my knapsack ahead. On the other side I stayed low and sprinted perhaps a hundred meters before stopping to catch my breath. After a few minutes I took another compass reading and started walking on that heading."

Kolev said he had not walked more than ten minutes when a voice close by called, 'Halt!' He stopped, and was surrounded by soldiers. One took him by the arm and guided him behind a stand of trees where someone turned a flashlight on his face. Then an officer stepped forward, and softly in Bulgarian, said, 'We've been waiting for you. Please fall in with these soldiers. We'll lead you.'

They had walked for perhaps a half an hour, with no further conversation, before coming to a shelter with a roof and three walls—a shepherd's lean-to. As they approached, Kolev could see a lantern and men in the shelter. The Americans were there, along with two Greek officers. The Americans greeted him warmly and embraced him, and the Greek officers shook hands. With only a few words exchanged, they left the lean-to and walked about a hundred meters to a jeep.

"The Americans put me in the back seat of the jeep, and with the Bulgarian driving, we took off."

"What did the Americans ask you once you were in the jeep?" Markov asked.

"Well, the Bulgarian said nothing, but the first thing the American asked for was my weapon, and he unloaded it and put the pistol in his belt. On the road, the American said they were very pleased to have me back, and asked if I was all right, and how the mission went. I told them it went well, but that I was unable to get the photographs because of the Bulgarian military vehicles parked in front of the site. The American turned and stared at me when I said that, but said nothing. They then asked if I was tired, and whether there were any unexpected incidents during my mission. I told them nothing happened that they hadn't trained me for, and that the mission was exciting, and if they wished, I would go on more missions. They said nothing after that; they didn't even speak to each other.

"I hoped with all my heart that I sounded convincing. My life depended on it."

Chapter 9

▼

The sun was well up, Kolev said said, before the jeep reached the outskirts of Kavalla. They drove through the town and took the road leading south along the coast, heading for the house on the beach where Kolev had stayed before. When they arrived, Petros, grinning widely, his teeth sparkling, came running and put both arms around Kolev, lifted him off the ground and swung him around. Petros kissed him on the cheek, and with a deep and hearty laugh, said, "Welcome home, my little warrior. I said prayers for you, and they have been answered. Look what we have prepared for you."

There, just off the veranda, a shallow pit had been dug and filled with burning charcoal. A Greek driver slowly turned a small goat on a spit over the coals. On the veranda a white cloth covered a table that held two large carafes of wine packed in ice buckets and two bottles of ouzo. Four chairs were spaced around the table.

The Bulgarian had taken several photographs of Kolev. One was a close-up of his face.

"After I showered and changed my clothes, we sat at the table, the Americans, Petros and I, and Petros poured each of us a glass of ouzo and put ice and a little water in each. Petros then stood, did a little dance step, and holding his glass at arm's length, said, 'Stand up!' We all stood. Petros said, 'A toast. We have among us a former boy who has joined the world of men. It is a thing to rejoice, and a thing to drink to, because men drink together. To hell with all the damned communists,' and with a laugh, he drained his glass with one swallow. We did, too, and then he grabbed the bottle and refilled all our glasses as we sat down."

The Bulgarian then had begun taking everything out of Kolev's knapsack, and had started glancing over the entries he had made in his notebook.

Kolev said the American turned to the Bulgarian, and said, "Hey—later." The Bulgarian returned to the table.

Petros shot a quick glance at both of them, his eyes questioning.

"We had no serious conversation that day. The American said we would relax and celebrate, and start work the next day, after I had had a night to sleep.

"Well, I'll tell you Mister Markov, we had a party. We really had a party!"

"The Americans did not appear to be suspicious of you it seems," Markov said.

"No, not at all," Kolev answered, nodding his head.

"We had many ouzos, and I had never seen Petros so talkative. He told stories and laughed more then I had ever seen him, and he kept patting me on the cheek and mussing my hair.

"The goat was soon ready, and it was delicious, the best I've ever had. It was basted in olive oil and lemon and stuffed with feta cheese, and we had a grand meal with the goat, salad and several loaves of bread, washing it down with glass after glass of cold retsina wine.

"About sunset I was getting very tired, and the ouzo and wine didn't help to keep me awake. I'd been up all night, but nevertheless, we partied on.

"The Bulgarian went into the house and brought out a radio that played music tapes, and with the volume as loud as possible, he played Greek bouzouki music.

"We began to dance, all in a line, with the lead dancer holding a handkerchief, the other end held by the person behind him in line. All in the line held hands. You know the dance; it's like ours. The Greeks call it the '*Sirtaki.*' When Petros was dancing on the end of the handkerchief, with me on the other end, he did such gyrations, turning in the air, and suddenly dropping down in a crouch on one foot and spinning around, that I kept losing my balance, and we all fell several times. Each time we all roared with laughter, and started all over again. Twice we fell off the veranda.

"The rest of the party I don't remember. I woke about midday the next day, lying on my bed with all my clothes on. My mouth was dry and I had a headache. When I got up, the Americans and Petros were sitting on the veranda, drinking coffee.

"They told me to shower and to eat, and Petros made coffee and a plate of eggs for me. When I finished eating, we moved inside to the table where they had put three chairs. Petros went outside.

"The Americans spread a large map on the table of the area where I'd been, and began questioning me about the route I'd walked. They went over it in such detail that I felt they wanted to know almost every step I had taken—that's an exaggeration—but they questioned me at great length about my route.

"Using my notebook, they matched my route with the recordings of azimuths I shot. They wanted to be sure that if I took an azimuth to an object that I was at a certain point on my route. That part was very difficult for me, and I got very confused at times, because as you know, I hadn't walked the route. When I got confused, they seemed irritated and they would question me more rapidly."

"Did they become suspicious? Did they realize you were lying to them?" Markov asked.

"Yes, I think they got suspicious at times, but eventually I convinced them I was telling the truth. You see, this questioning went on for several days. That first session lasted all day and well into the night, until after midnight.

"From time to time we would take a break, and walk out to the veranda and smoke a cigarette. When we did, Petros would go in the house and prepare sandwiches for us. We drank nothing but water."

The next morning Petros had awakened Kolev at six, and the Americans were already there, sitting at the table. Again they questioned Kolev all day and into the night, and did so for three days. It was a grueling, difficult period for Kolev, because the Americans had conducted those kinds of debriefings before, and their questions came quickly, going over the same subjects repeatedly to make sure they got the same answers each time.

"I was greatly relieved when the sessions ended," Kolev said, shaking his head and resting his chin in the palm of one hand, his fingers covering his mouth.

"How did they end?" Markov asked, watching Kolev closely.

"Well, on the third evening they suddenly stopped the questioning and shook my hand, and then started a long discussion about my future.

"Throughout the questioning I had repeatedly made comments about my willingness to go on future missions—but trying to be subtle—and let them know that if they'd pay me for each mission I would soon have enough money to resettle in the West with a nest egg that would permit me a better start in a new country. I told them my life's ambition was to resettle in America, and that I hoped I could use my time in Greece to learn English."

"Did they give you English lessons?" Markov interrupted.

"No, I picked up quite a bit of Greek living with Petros, but the Americans said that when the time came they would see that I was given proper English lessons in a language school."

"What happened then?"

"Nothing, for a long time. I lived at the house with Petros for almost five months, and we did nothing but swim and lounge around the house. It was very boring. Once in a while Petros and the driver would take me to Drama for a dinner, but that was seldom."

"Did they give you any physical training? Were there no hikes with Petros?" Markov asked.

"No, we did nothing." Kolev said. "The Americans came by the house every week or ten days, just to talk"

There was a long silence.

"But then they dispatched you back to Bulgaria on another mission," Markos said. "Didn't they care about your physical conditioning for that mission?" he asked, Kolev, his eyebrows raised.

"No, because they said the next mission would not be physically challenging, that I didn't have to be in great physical condition because there would be very little strenuous walking involved."

"So, as I understand it, you did nothing for almost five months, and then they came and offered you another mission. Is that what you're telling me?" Markov asked.

"Yes, sir," Kolev said, looking at his hands.

"Tell me about your preparation for the next mission." Markov said.

"Well, the Americans had arrived at the house one evening just after Petros and I finished dinner, and we sat on the veranda and had coffee and a brandy. The American said they had given my future a great deal of thought, and that they were willing to send me on another mission. They would pay me five thousand dollars if I completed that mission successfully, and would pay me five thousand dollars for each following mission. When I had no further interest in going on missions, they would resettle me in America with their support.

"I asked what the mission would be.

"They said that if I agreed with the offer, they would return in a day or so and give me the details and begin briefing me on how to carry it out.

"Right then I agreed to go on another mission, and told them I was very pleased about being given five thousand dollars. With that they departed."

"What did Petros say about you going on another mission?" Markov asked.

"He didn't seem to know anything about it, but I told him they had asked me to go on another mission." Kolev paused, glancing down again, he said, "He just looked at me and shrugged, and said something like, 'You can do it.'

"Two days later, the Americans arrived at the house in the morning. We sat at the table and with maps, train and bus schedules; they briefed me. As usual, Petros stayed on the veranda."

"What was the mission?" Markov asked.

The Americans had told Kolev of a factory located four kilometers south of Ruse, at number 79 Seven November Road. A high stone fence surrounded the factory, with double iron gates at the entrance to the compound, and a guard always at the gate. Beyond the gates was a large courtyard, and on the far side the entrance to a dark gray, two-story dilapidated building. But the building was a plant where one-to-twenty-five-thousand scale maps of Greece and Turkey were produced. The maps were used to coordinate targeting of intermediate range missiles from the Soviet Union.

"They wanted me to obtain a complete set of maps for both Greece and Turkey and bring them out. I thought they were joking. I asked how in the world I was going to get inside that building and get copies of the maps."

The director of the plant, they had told Kolev, was a man named Dimitri Atanasov, who would know about Kolev's mission and expect him. Kolev would cross the border at night as before, carrying a knapsack containing Bulgarian documentation, food, clean underwear, dress shoes, dress slacks, shirt, necktie, jacket, shaving gear and briefcase. After crossing the border, Kolev would change into those clothes, hide the knapsack and take the briefcase with him. In the briefcase he would carry the food, underwear, shaving gear and documentation: a Bulgarian identity card showing that his name was Ivan Vasilev, a lieutenant in the missile forces. He would also carry military orders authorizing him to travel from Sofia to Ruse on military business. At the gates of the factory he was to present his identity card and ask to speak to Mister Atanasov, and the guard would let him enter and direct him to the entrance of the factory. When he entered the building, he would show a receptionist his identity card and tell her that he had an appointment with Mr. Atanasov.

"They said Mister Atanasov would come to the reception area, greet me and escort me to a meeting room off the reception area, and ask me if I had any further identification. I was to tell him that Dimitrios sent me and show him half of a playing card, the ace of spades. Upon seeing the card, they said, Mister Atanasov would excuse himself and return with a briefcase, and we would exchange briefcases. Atanasov's would be the same color and size as mine and it would contain a newspaper from Ruse, magazines, a small loaf of salami and some bread. I was to put the few items from my brief case into the new briefcase. They explained, however, that the brief case Atanasov would give me would have a false bottom, and in a cavity, the two sets of maps.

"Mister Atanasov, they said, would also give me an address in Ruse and the name of the family there, and after leaving the factory I would go to that address. The family would expect me and would feed me and put me up for the night. They told me to leave the next day and travel through Sofia to the border area and there recover my knapsack, change my clothes and cross the border at the same point I had crossed on the way in.

"We talked about what I was to do almost the entire day."

The next day, Kolev said, he was briefed by the Americans as to where he would cross the border and how he would proceed to Ruse. They told him they would put him across the border about five kilometers east of Kulata, and would make certain the fence would be easy to cross, as before. He had to walk two hours north after crossing, and then turn west and walk toward the road from Kulata to Sandanski. But before reaching the road, he should change clothes and hide the knapsack. When he reached the road he would be in the vicinity of a roadhouse where the bus to Sofia stopped. They instructed him to eat breakfast and linger there long enough to catch an afternoon bus. The bus ride to Sofia would take about four hours, and would arrive at the Ovcha Kupel terminal on Tsar Boris III Street. From there he was to take a tram to the Central Train Station.

"They told me to buy a ticket on the midnight train to Ruse as soon as I arrived at the station, and then to go to a small restaurant across the street from the train station, eat dinner and stay in that restaurant until time to board the train. 'Don't stay in the station waiting around for your train,' they said. At night the underground passageways were full of derelicts and teenage criminals, and the police often raided the area. They assured me that the documents they would give me would pass any police inspection, but they still did not want me questioned by the police."

"They seemed to know Sofia in some detail, but they obviously had people in their embassy in Sofia who had learned the city well," Markov said.

"Well, they certainly knew more about many things in Bulgaria than I did," Kolev said.

Markov stood and stretched, and reached for the pack of cigarettes on the table, but the pack was empty. He went to the door, opened it, stepped into the hallway and called the guard. The guard must have been sitting close by, because he came immediately. Markov asked him to bring a pack of cigarettes, then came back into the room. "I was wondering when you were going to notice that,"

Kolev said. Markov chuckled, and said, "You smoke too much." Within a few minutes, the guard opened the door and handed cigarettes to Markov, who opened the pack, offered a cigarette to Kolev, took one for himself, and lit both.

"Go on. And then what?" Markov said as he sat.

"I don't have much more to say about the mission. They told me I would arrive in Ruse the next morning, and that I should shave and clean up before getting off the train. They said to eat breakfast and then take a taxi to the factory. Do you want me to tell you what my instructions were after I got the maps, how I was to return to Greece?"

"No. That won't be necessary, since it never happened. Go on with what actually happened." Markov said.

"Well, off and on for two days we went over and over the mission so that I would remember everything, because they didn't want me to take any notes.

"Then they didn't appear for two days, but on the third day they arrived early in the morning and told me that I would be leaving that night. All morning we went over the map, and they showed me where I would cross the border, what compass heading I should follow and for how long, and showed me where I should be at that point, because there I was to turn east and head for the Kulata road. They also showed me on the map the location of the roadhouse where I would eat and catch the bus to Sofia.

"That afternoon I rested. About nine that evening they came for me, and I could see that the American again had a pistol in a shoulder holster under his jacket. They had a shotgun in the front seat of the jeep."

"Did they give you a weapon?" Markov asked.

"No. But, to appear authentic, I asked where my weapon was. They said I wouldn't need one since, except for crossing the border, all of my travel would be overt."

"That's strange," Markov said, "because crossing the border is the most dangerous part."

"I thought so too, but they didn't give me one," Kolev said.

"Okay, then what?" Markov asked.

"Well, we drove through Kavalla and west through Drama, and then turned north toward the border, and sometime after midnight, while driving on a dirt road, a light flashed ahead of us. We came to a halt and a Greek army officer and several soldiers approached. The officer had a jeep and there was a truck with some more Greek soldiers in it. The American talked to the officer and within a few minutes the officer got in his jeep. We followed, and behind us came the truck of soldiers. After about an hour, we were climbing slowly all the time, we stopped, and the soldiers got out of the truck and started walking toward the border. It was pitch black, not a light anywhere. At some point the Greek officer talked into a radio, left his jeep, came back to ours, and said, '*Pes ton na elthi.*' The American told me to get out of the jeep and follow the officer. The Americans shook hands with me and I fell in behind the officer. After we had walked maybe half a kilometer, we stopped and a Greek soldier approached us out of the darkness. The officer spoke to him, and the soldier turned to me and in Bulgarian said that we were approximately one hundred meters from the border. He told me to go forward from there and cross the border, and they would cover me. I thanked him and started toward the border.

"At the border fence the lower strand of wire was loose. I got under the wire with my knapsack and crossed without difficulty. About twenty meters beyond the fence I encountered a dirt road, which I guessed was used by border guards to patrol by vehicle. I headed east on it. After about thirty minutes, I saw headlights approaching, and as the vehicle got nearer, I stood in the middle of the road waving my arms. It was a border guard jeep. When it stopped a few meters from me, three soldiers jumped out and pointed weapons at me, shouting for me to raise my hands. They asked for my identity and demanded to know what I was doing there. I told them I wanted to see their commanding officer at once, but they kept repeating their questions, and I kept saying that I wanted to see their commanding officer. Then they searched me and went through my knapsack, put handcuffs on me and put me in the back of the jeep.

"They turned and drove east, and we soon arrived at the border guard post. Several soldiers were hanging around outside the building, and the soldiers with me told them they had caught me at the border. They handled me roughly, dragging me from the jeep and pushing me toward the building. Inside they made me sit in a chair at a desk. No officer was in the room, although there were many soldiers. I sat there for perhaps ten minutes and no one spoke. I didn't say a word. Finally, a captain walked in from a back door. The soldiers jumped to attention. I stayed in the chair because it was difficult for me to jump up with my hands cuffed behind my back. A soldier told the captain that they had captured me at the border, that he had searched me and my belongings, and that I appeared to him to be a border crosser, but I had no weapon.

"The officer turned to me and asked, 'Who are you?'

"I told the officer that if I could have my hands freed I'd write who I was for his eyes only. He hesitated for a moment, but then ordered the handcuffs removed and pushed a writing pad and a pen toward me. He pulled his pistol from his holster and laid it on the desk in front of me. I wrote the telephone number the colonel had given me to memorize, and wrote also that he should telephone that number and say, 'Tell Hakim the oak tree has fallen.'

"The officer studied me for a few moments and then ordered all the soldiers to leave the room. When the room was cleared, he said, 'I will do nothing until you tell me who you are and why I should place this telephone call.'

"I told him I was on a mission for the Bulgarian Government and the message I had asked him to send would go to a very important colonel in Sofia. He nodded, and said, 'If you're lying you're a dead man.'

"I said, 'Please, place the call.'

"The officer dialed the number and repeated the message I had given him. He waited a long time—perhaps five minutes or so—then, obviously the person on the other end of the line gave instructions to him, because he hung up, reached for his pistol and replaced it in his holster. He told me that someone from Sofia would come to pick me up within five hours. He then called a soldier and told him to put me in a room, to make me comfortable and have food sent to me.

"They took me to a nice room, probably the sleeping room of an officer, and in a very few minutes, one of them brought food. Immediately after eating I lay on the bed and fell asleep without taking off my clothes."

Kolev said he was awakened in the morning by a captain who shook him gently and told him to wash up because they were leaving for Sofia in a few minutes. Outside, they put him in the back of a jeep, with the captain and a driver in the front. It was shortly after dawn.

They had driven to Sofia without a word spoken, and did not go to the building to which Kolev had been taken the last time, but instead went to the eastern suburbs and pulled up in front of a gate to a large villa. No guard was visible, but as they stopped, a man in civilian clothes appeared and opened the gate. They drove in and parked in front of the villa. The captain escorted Kolev to the front door, where the colonel stood, dressed in a dark blue blazer and gray slacks, with an ascot at his throat. The colonel gave Kolev a big embrace; almost lifting him off his feet, and laughing loudly, told Kolev he was very excited to see him again. The captain left.

The colonel patted Kolev on the back, put his arm around his shoulders and led him to a bar in a den adjacent to the living room. There he poured two brandies in large snifters, and from a pot he poured two cups of coffee. Placing the drinks on a coffee table, the colonel motioned for Kolev to sit on the sofa behind the table, and the colonel sat on a chair next to the table, handing Kolev a brandy. After clinking glasses, the colonel raised his glass and said, "Welcome home, my boy, I knew you could do it." He banged a hand on the table and threw back half the brandy. Kolev joined him, but choked and coughed. The brandy burned. The colonel asked Kolev when he had to be back in Greece, and when Kolev said he had to be at the border in five nights, the colonel nodded and said, "Good, that is plenty of time."

When they had finished their drinks, the colonel clapped his hands and told Kolev a hot bath awaited him upstairs. An orderly appeared and asked Kolev to follow him.

"I had never seen such a room. It was as big as my father's house, and for that matter, I had never been in such a house. I thought kings must live in such places. The orderly pointed to fresh clothes on the bed, gave me a robe, and said that at the end of the hall was a bath waiting for me, and that after I had bathed and dressed, I should return to the lower level to join the colonel.

"You should have seen that bathroom, Mister Markov. There was a large tub filled with hot water, a sink and a mirror, a razor and soap to shave with, and several wonderfully smelling colognes that I could put on myself after I bathed. They had six, actually six big thick towels hanging on racks that one could use to dry off. I thought how exciting it was to be treated as a hero in your own country. That was a wonderful welcome."

Kolev slumped in his chair, his shoulders sagged, and he pulled out his handkerchief, and blew his nose, and dabbed his eyes with the heel of his right hand.

"After I bathed I returned to the sleeping room and noticed that my clothes were gone, so I put on the new clothes and went down to join the colonel, who led me to a large dining room. It must have been a banquet hall. There was a table with twelve chairs, and the colonel and I sat opposite each other, and the orderly served us breakfast, just the two of us. And what a meal it was. We had orange juice, beef, eggs, fried cheese, yogurt, bread, fruit, coffee and another large brandy. I'll never forget that meal. It was the last good meal I ever had.

"As we ate, the colonel questioned me about my reception in Greece after my last mission. I told him everything I could think of about the questions the Americans had asked me, telling him how carefully they questioned me about my route, my compass readings and my notes."

"What did they say about your failure to take the photographs?" he asked.

"I told him they said nothing, that they seemed to treat it as a stroke of bad luck. His questions about what happened in Greece went on long after we had finished our meal.

"We then went to another room that had large leather chairs and sofas. The walls were covered with books. There the colonel questioned me about what I had learned about the Americans. I had very little to tell him about them, because they told me nothing about themselves. He seemed disappointed, and asked me if they gave me English lessons. I told him that they said they would give me proper English lessons after I resettled in the West. Then, speaking in Greek, he asked me if I had learned any Greek. I was surprised that he could speak Greek, and in Bulgarian I told him I had picked up some words from Petros, but that Petros and I usually spoke in Bulgarian. He could tell I hadn't learned much Greek. He also seemed surprised that the Americans saw me very little for almost five months, and that they left me with Petros so long with nothing to do, but he said he was pleased the Americans had agreed to pay me five thousand dollars for each mission."

During that discussion, Kolev said, there were long pauses during which the colonel studied him without saying anything.

"Although I could tell he was not entirely satisfied with what had happened to me after I returned to Greece, I could think of nothing to explain why not much had happened there.

"He then turned to my new mission and took detailed notes about everything I told him. His eyes opened wide, and he jerked his head back when I told him I had to meet a man named Atanasov at a map factory in Ruse, and that a family in Ruse would take me in for the night.

"When I finished telling him that, he went to another room and I heard him talking on a telephone, saying the name Atanasov, and mentioning maps. He told someone to bring Atanasov to Sofia with the briefcase. 'I want to know how he got it.'

"When he returned to the room I heard a ringing sound, and the orderly went to the front door. He then came to our room and gave the colonel the military identification card and the military orders that the Americans had given me. The colonel was angry that the Americans were able to produce Bulgarian documents so well, and he cursed and threw them on the floor.

"We talked for several more hours about my mission, and he wanted to know everything the Americans told me about the maps and Atanasov. Then a very strange thing happened. I heard the ringing sound again, and when the orderly went to the front door, I heard several voices, and then the orderly came to our room and told the colonel some officers wished to see him immediately.

"The colonel yelled at the orderly that he was not to be disturbed. The orderly left. But then a man in civilian clothes entered and said, 'Forgive me, my colonel, but we have something you must see. It is of the utmost importance.' The colonel cursed, left the room with the man, and I could hear muffled voices. They talked for quite some time.

"Then the colonel returned to our room with two men in civilian clothes. I remember one of the men clearly; he had a pockmarked face and a large scar running down his left cheek. He stared coldly at me, and his eyes had no expression. He was a tough looking man, and I would see more of him later. The colonel handed me half of a foreign currency bill, and opened a piece of silver paper containing four frames of exposed film. The colonel asked, 'What was on these frames of film before the silver paper was opened and exposed them, and why did you have this?' He was pointing to the half of a bill.

"I didn't know what the colonel was talking about, and I said, 'I have never seen those. I don't know what they are.'

"The colonel's voice was rising. 'This is half of an American five-dollar bill. Where did you get it? Who is it for? Were you to give these to Atanasov? Or is there another part of your mission that you have not told me about? What was on this film?'

"I said, 'Colonel, I swear to you, I have never seen those things,. I did not bring them with me!'

"The colonel slapped me hard in the face and shouted, 'You lying bastard, you're doubled! You're under the control of the Americans. I'll have you shot.' I repeated over and over again that I didn't know what those things were, and that I didn't bring them with me. The colonel slapped me two more times, almost knocking me out of the chair."

The colonel had turned to the two men in civilian clothes, and said, "Take him away and get the truth out of him." The scar-faced man grabbed Kolev out of the chair, and the other man put handcuffs on him with his hands behind his back. They pushed him out of the room and out the front door of the house and threw him into the back seat of a civilian automobile.

"I never saw the colonel again. And then began the worst ordeal of my life."

Chapter 10

The two men had driven Kolev to the same building where the colonel had taken him the first time he entered Bulgaria from Greece. Inside, in the reception room, they gave him to two armed guards who took him directly to a cell that contained only a cot and one chair. A guard freed his hands and made him strip, giving him a gray jumpsuit and a pair of rubber sandals. They took his clothes and watch, and gave him one towel and a bar of soap, then left, locking him in.

"A couple of hours later the guards came for me. I'm just guessing about the time—in that cell I never knew what time it was, because the cell had no window, and a light bulb suspended from the ceiling stayed lit all the time. I lost all track of time. It was terrible not to know whether it was day or night. But I wasn't there long when the guards took me to an interrogation room, and put me in a chair in front of a desk. It was dark in the room except for one desk lamp, directed at my face. I could see that two men were sitting behind the desk, but I couldn't make out their features because of the light in my eyes. They were just shadows.

"One man got up and came around the desk. He was smoking a cigarette, and he grabbed me by the hair and started to put his cigarette out on my cheek. I yelled. It burned terribly. I grabbed his hand, but he broke loose, dropped the cigarette, and hit me in the mouth with his fist. I was stunned. I could see blood running down the front of my jumpsuit. The man bent over and put his face close to mine. It was the scar-faced man. He said, 'If you ever touch me again I'll kill you,' and returned to a chair behind the desk.

"He said, 'Kolev you have lied to us. No one in the world knows where you are, and we'll do with you whatever we wish, and no one will ever know. Can you comprehend that?'

"I said, 'Yes, sir, but please, I have *not* lied to you, I don't know where those things came from. I had never seen them until the colonel showed them to me.' I could feel my lips swelling."

Kolev said the second man got up from his chair and walked around the desk. He had something in his hand, and he held it in the light so Kolev could see it. It was about one meter long, and appeared to be three thick leather thongs woven together. It probably had been soaked in water, because it was stiff and hard. He moved back out of the light and suddenly struck Kolev hard across his thighs with the rod. Kolev didn't see the blow coming, and the pain was excruciating. He screamed and bent over, and the man struck him across the back, driving the breath out of him, and he fell from the chair, unconscious.

"When I came to I was again sitting in the chair, in terrible pain. It hurt to breathe. The man with the rod was still standing beside me.

"The scar-faced man asked, 'Where did you get the half of an American five-dollar bill, to whom were you instructed to show it? What was on the film before it was exposed? To whom were you instructed to give it?'"

The man's voice had been hoarse, his words clipped, and spoken rapidly.

"I said, 'Please, sir, you must believe me. I've never seen those things before, and I can't make up some reason to give you.' The man with the rod hit me again on the thighs, and when I bent over, he hit me across the back. Everything went gray and I fell out of the chair.

"This went on for hours, the same questions, the same blows with the rod. I came to on my cot in the cell, and someone had placed a glass of water and a bowl of cold beans on the table. I gulped the water down, but my lips were so swollen, and I was so sore that eating was difficult. But I did eat the beans. I had no idea what time it was or even what day, but a guard looked into my cell, and when he saw me awake he came in and led me to the bathroom and then back to my cell. Shortly after, the guards came again and took me back to the interrogation room."

Kolev stood, put his hands to his head, swaying forward as he remembered. He straightened, and said, "Mister Markov, that beating was horrible. No human being should ever experience it. I didn't have an answer to their questions." He sat, put his head in his hands and sobbed.

Markov waited, his eyes filling with tears. After a few moments, his voice cracking, he said: "Go on, if you can."

Kolev sat for long moments, studying his hands. He then cleared his throat, and said, "Well, from behind the desk the scar-faced man said, 'Kolev, we're going to ask you the same questions again, and if you don't answer them truthfully there will be the same consequences, because we have orders to beat you to death if you don't tell us the truth.'

"I said, 'Please tell me where you found those items, perhaps if I knew where they were I could tell you how they got there.'

"The scar-faced man said, 'Those items were sent with you to Bulgaria, and if they were sent here with you, you were obviously to use them here, and if you were to use them in Bulgaria, you know where they were. Kolev, are you really prepared to sacrifice your life to serve the Americans? If you are, we're going to accommodate you, so tell me where you got half of an American five-dollar bill, and why you had it.'

"I, of course, couldn't answer. So, the beating began again. I don't know how many times I fell from the chair, and it seemed to go on forever. Again I woke up on my cot in the cell. It seemed to me that the guards would check my cell frequently, and if they found me asleep they would awaken me and take me to the interrogation room where the beatings would start again. I have no idea how long this went on, but I remember that I became unable to talk. Sitting in the chair in the interrogation room, I could think of something to say but realized I was making sounds that nobody could understand. I wanted to die, and I thought of ways to kill myself, but I couldn't find anything to use. There was nothing in my cell I could use to hang myself, and nothing to cut myself."

"Kolev," Markov said, "at your trial these two items, the half of the five-dollar bill, and the exposed film, were used as major points by the prosecutor to convict you. Is it *really* possible that you didn't know you had them with you when you crossed the border?"

"Mister Markov, I wouldn't have gone through those beatings if I could have explained where those two things came from. I've always thought that the Bulgarian government didn't really find them in my belongings, that they created them as an excuse to convict me. I don't know why they would've done that to me. Perhaps they wanted a spy trial for some political reason, and I just happened to be the one they chose to use as an example. But I was serving them loyally, and I thought the mission I had carried out was important for the government. No, Mister Markov, to this day I can't explain those two items. I know they weren't with me."

"Go on, tell me what happened next."

"Well, the interrogations and the beatings finally stopped, and I was fed a proper meal and allowed to bathe. They also moved me to another cell, a larger one with two cots, one over the other. What seemed like four or five days later, the door opened and another prisoner was pushed into the cell. He was about my age, tall and nice looking, and he spoke as if he were well-educated."

"Who was he?"

The man had told Kolev that his name was Khristo Dimitrov. He said he was from Sofia and that he had been a student at the University of Sofia, but had been expelled for activities against the state. Kolev asked him what kind of activities, and the man said he had spoken openly against the Communist regime among his fellow students, and that there were lots of students at the university who were against the Communists. Most were afraid to talk openly. "Only when you get to know them well, and they trust you, will they discuss their true beliefs," he had said.

Dimitrov said that after he was expelled from school he joined an anti-Communist underground group that published leaflets and tracts and distributed them clandestinely. The group also tried to make contact with western countries to ask for money and other support to help their cause. He personally had gone to the British Embassy and asked to speak with someone who would be interested in helping an anti-Communist underground organization. But the British had told him there was no such person in the Embassy and had asked him to leave. Somehow the security services learned about his activities and had arrested him a week earlier. He said he had been under interrogation since then and had been beaten to make him reveal the names of others in his underground group. He claimed that he had given them no names, that he would never betray his friends.

"Oh, for God's sake, that's so blatant—did you believe him?" Markov asked.

"Yeah, I did, but he didn't look to me as if he had been beaten. But then I had no obvious signs I'd been beaten either. Though I still had deep bruises on my thighs and back, there wasn't a mark on my face. My lips had healed. But I didn't see any bruises on his body."

"What did you tell him to explain why you were in prison?"

"I eventually told him that I had been sent on a mission to Greece by the Bulgarian Intelligence Service to allow myself to be recruited by the Americans, and be sent back to Bulgaria on an espionage mission for them. And when I came back to Bulgaria, to report everything I had learned. I told him I had succeeded and was actually sent back to Bulgaria on a mission for the Americans.

"He asked, 'Then why are you in a prison cell? Didn't you tell them?' I told him I had, but for some reason they didn't believe me, and I didn't know why.

He then asked, 'If the Americans knew you were in here do you think they'd try to help you?' I said they probably would as long as they didn't know I had been reporting to the Bulgarian Intelligence Service.

"At that point he became very excited, and asked, 'Do you know how to make contact with the Americans? If you do, I can help you.'

"I said, 'Look Khristo, you and I are in the same cell; we couldn't make contact with our own mothers if we wanted to, much less the Americans.'"

Markov shook his head, pointed his finger at Kolev, and said, "That man, Khristo, if he were serious, would have had to be extraordinarily naïve, and perhaps recklessly dangerous."

"Well, I'll tell you more about him, but he said, 'No, no, you're wrong, if you know of some way to contact the Americans in Bulgaria, I can help you, trust me, I won't betray you. I have trusted friends in my organization, and I could pass them whatever message you want, and they will do what you ask. My organization would do anything to make contact with the Americans. My fiancée will be allowed to visit me here, and she'll do anything I ask. She can be counted on to carry any message you want to send out.'

"I told him I had no way to contact the Americans unless I was sent back to Greece. But he kept after me about this, and I don't think he believed me. Finally, he gave up and stopped talking about it. Later, they took him out of my cell."

"Did you ever see him again?" Markov asked.

"Oh, yes. I saw him again all right. He testified against me at my trial. On the witness stand he testified that we'd been cellmates, and that I had confided to him that I was supposed to make contact with a man named Anatoli Gronsky in Sofia. He said I told him that I was to pass Gronsky half of an American five-dollar bill to identify myself, and then to pass him frames of film concealed in silver paper. He also testified that I asked him if he had any way to get a message to Gronsky"

"Who was Anatoli Gronsky? You haven't mentioned that name?"

"I have no idea," Kolev said, "I'd never heard that name until he mentioned it on the witness stand."

"Why do you think he testified to such information about you?" Markov asked.

"Well, I think it's obvious. Since I wasn't able to tell them how I got the five-dollar bill and the film, they didn't have much to go on to convict me, so they used Dimitrov, or whatever his name was, to help convince the court that I was guilty."

"Did the colonel testify at your trial?"

"No, as I said, I never saw the colonel after I was taken from the villa to the prison. The scar-faced man didn't testify either."

"How long did you have to wait for your trial to begin?" Markov asked.

Kolev shrugged, opened both hands palms up, thought for a moment, and said, "I don't know exactly."

But about a month after the man called Dimitrov had left his cell, Kolev was taken to an interrogation room where two men were waiting. They said they were prosecutors, and the senior of the two told Kolev that he was going to put him on trial and charge him with espionage. He said he would ask for the death penalty. Kolev tried to explain that he didn't commit espionage against Bulgaria and tried to tell the prosecutor all that he had been through while trying to serve his country. But the prosecutor had no interest. It was a waste of time.

"Then I realized that the prosecutor was going to put me on trial no matter what I said, because, he said, 'You'll have a defense lawyer, tell him your side of the story. It's not my job to listen to it.' I asked him when the trial would start, and he said, 'You'll be told.' Then they left.

"About three weeks later I was again taken to an interrogation room, and there I met a man named Georgi Milev, a mousy little man with no chin and a little black moustache. He told me he was going to be my defense attorney. I asked him when the trial was going to start.

"He said, 'Tomorrow.' Mister Milev asked me to tell him the entire story about where this all began, and how I had ended up there. So I told him why I escaped to Greece and how, about being coerced by the Americans to come to Bulgaria on an espionage mission, and how I turned myself in. I went through the details of my conversations with the colonel and that I had agreed to return to Greece to penetrate the American cross-border program. I emphasized how successful I was in doing that. I told him also that when I returned from that mission, the colonel didn't believe that I'd told him the truth.

"Mister Milev said, 'Tell me about the American currency and the film you had with you.'

"I tried to explain to him, as I had to everyone, that I knew nothing about those things and hadn't seen them until the colonel showed them to me. Milev got angry, and said, 'Come now, Mister Kolev, you must be honest with me if I am to defend you. What you say to me will be held in the strictest confidence.' He asked me the name of the colonel, and I told him I didn't know. In short, Mister Markov, we didn't have a very good conversation. After about an hour

Mister Milev left, and as he left he said, 'Kolev you'll be convicted. If I am totally successful tomorrow I'll save you from the death penalty.'"

Kolev leaned back, took a cigarette from the pack, lit it and inhaled deeply. He looked up as he exhaled and for long moments said nothing. Then he threw the cigarette on the floor and stomped on it.

He told Markov that the next morning he was taken in handcuffs out of the prison and driven to the court. Two guards had escorted him to a large courtroom where they ordered him to sit on a chair at the side. The chair was in a small enclosure bordered by a low wooden railing. Guards sat behind him. Behind a long high desk sat three judges, and behind them four large windows reached almost to the high ceiling, each framed by thick, black drapes. In front of the judges' desk were two smaller desks. with the two prosecutors behind one, and Kolev's attorney behind the other. There was no one else in the room. Milev, Kolev's attorney, didn't look at Kolev or acknowledge his presence.

One of the judges had asked the prosecutor to read the charges against Kolev.

"I don't remember all the words, but he said things like, "crime of espionage against the people," and "traitorous acts on behalf of an imperialist power," and "providing false statements to the Peoples' Representative Authorities," and on and on. He ended by stating that the state demanded the death penalty. When he finished the judge asked, 'How does the defendant plead?' Without looking at me, Mister Milev said, 'The defendant pleads guilty with extenuating circumstances.' I tried to speak, but one of the judges told me to shut up, and told the prosecutor to proceed."

The prosecutor had stood and stated that Kolev had a record of unsatisfactory performance at the collective where he had worked, that he left Bulgaria illegally, had agreed to be recruited by the intelligence service of an imperialist power, and had entered Bulgaria illegally on an espionage mission for that service. He offered as evidence testimony made by the director of the collective and Kolev's own statements from conversations he had had with the colonel.

The prosecutor said that in an attempt to rehabilitate Kolev the security service of the Peoples' Republic had given him a chance to redeem himself, and had offered to let him return abroad and work for the Peoples' Republic against the intelligence service of the imperialist power. He continued that Kolev was subsequently dispatched again to Bulgaria on another espionage mission on behalf of the foreign intelligence service. "But," he said, "when given the opportunity by the Peoples' security service to tell them the details of that mission, the defendant lied to the authorities and deliberately attempted to withhold information." He then offered as evidence the half of the American five-dollar bill, the exposed film, and the silver paper in which it had been wrapped. He said the authorities had found these items on Kolev and identified them as accoutrements of a clandestine operation. "The defendant," he said, "refused to cooperate to help identify the purpose for which they were intended."

"He then called as a witness my former cellmate. I was shocked to see him. He was dressed in a suit and necktie, while I still wore my gray prison jumpsuit. I told you the testimony he gave, but he told the court also that he was in prison in a case of mistaken identity and had asked to be removed from my cell because he found my constant ravings against the Communist Party and the Peoples' Republic repulsive. My attorney didn't ask him a single question, and Dimitrov was excused. The prosecutor summed up the case against me and sat down. The entire thing took about one hour."

The judge had called the prosecutor and Kolev's attorney to his desk. and the three whispered for a long time. The judge then adjourned the court for the day, and the guards took Kolev back to his cell.

The next morning Kolev again had been escorted to the courtroom, and the judge asked Kolev's attorney to present his defense. Milev said he was unable to alleviate the prosecutors' charges against Kolev, but asked the court to show him mercy, explaining that Kolev came from a humble background, from a hard-working family, and that he had served loyally in the army and had no prior criminal record. He stated also that Kolev's father's brother held a significant position in a regional Communist Party organization.

Milev had told the court that during the time he spent with Kolev preparing for his defense, he found Kolev to be naïve and impressionable, and believed those characteristics, rather than evil intent, led Kolev to that courtroom. He said it would serve no purpose to put Kolev to death, and he sat down.

The judge had ordered Kolev out of the courtroom, and the guards escorted him out to a small sitting room where they waited for about an hour. Then the door opened, and Kolev's guards were told to return him to the courtroom. When Kolev entered, the prosecutor and Kolev's attorney were talking with the judge, and when Kolev sat down, the attorneys returned to their desks. The judge turned to Kolev and said, "The defendant will rise." Kolev stood, his legs shaking. The judge said, "Prisoner Ivan Kolev, this court has found you guilty of the charges brought against you by the state. This court hereby sentences you to life in prison, with no provision for parole. Take the prisoner away."

"Well, Mister Markov," Kolev said, "that's the entire story, and that's Bulgarian justice for you. I didn't have a chance, but I guess that's why you're here. I think I've told you everything."

Markov scribbled for a few moments, and said, "I'm not an attorney, but it's possible that your trial was not held in violation of the law at that time. But I'm satisfied with what you've told me."

"Please, Mister Markov, I'm innocent," Kolev said. "I hope you can find someone who will believe me."

"As I explained to you when we began," Markov said, "my role is not to convince anyone to believe you. I'll enter your comments into the judicial review. That's all I can promise."

Markov rose, put his coat on, buttoned it, and walked around to face Kolev. Kolev stood and extended his hand, but Markov brushed it aside and embraced him, saying, "Ivan, I truly wish you good luck." The two men shook hands and Markov left. Kolev noticed that Markov had left the pack of cigarettes on the desk for him.

Part II

*Headquarters
Central Intelligence Agency
Langley, Virginia*

Chapter 1

▼

The entrance to the grounds of CIA headquarters in Langley, Virginia, leads to a massive, seven-story, white concrete building, connected by corridors and a courtyard to another large building at its rear. Sitting on over 200 acres, the grounds are landscaped with dogwoods, azaleas, oak and maple trees and lush green lawns. The ambiance is more that of a college campus than a government agency. Jogging trails abound.

Inside the entrance, inlaid in the marble floor, the circular seal of the CIA carries the words, "Central Intelligence Agency," spaced around the top half, and "United States of America," on a simulated scroll across the bottom. In the center the head of an American eagle rests on a shield and a compass rose, indicating the agency's international reach.

Carved in the marble wall on the left are the words, "And ye shall know the truth, and the truth shall make you free. John 8:32." Chiseled on the right wall, are rows of black stars, one for each life lost in the line of duty—most of them anonymous. Below the stars a glass-enclosed open book on a stand includes the names of Richard Welch, chief of station, Athens, Greece, shot to death in front of his home in 1975, and William Buckley, chief of station, Beirut, Lebanon, tortured to death in 1985. Above the stars are the engraved words, "In honor of those members of the Central Intelligence Agency who gave their lives in the service of their country."

On the fourth floor an intercom buzzed on the desk of Roger East, and the secretary said, "Mister East, Mister John Kelley from the Counter-Intelligence Staff has sent you a file he'd like you to review, and he'd like to come up tomorrow morning to discuss it with you."

"Good, bring it in and put him down for whatever time I have free in the morning."

Roger East, chief of the European Division of the Directorate of Operations, leaned back and thoughts of Jack Kelly flooded his mind. They came into the agency in the same class and had been through a lot together. Jack, a Yale graduate, had joined after a stint as a Green Beret officer in Vietnam. They had both served in Beirut, a difficult tour for both because they had been separated from their families.

Jack had been shot while he sat beside Roger in a CIA operational car, creeping along a dark street in the city's Moslem section.

Roger's chair began to tilt backwards, and he grabbed his desk with both hands to steady himself. He hated that chair but could not remember to tell his secretary to send for another.

As the secretary entered the office and placed the file on his desk, Roger looked out of windows that covered two walls of his office. It was a dark and blustery day; rain beat hard on the windows, casting dripping shadows on his wall. Behind his oversized mahogany desk stood two flags on stands, the Stars and Stripes and a blue flag with the CIA emblem.

Roger was a CIA brat, the son of a CIA officer. When Roger was five, his father had been assigned to Greece, and the family lived there seven years. Roger went to an American school, but all his neighbors were Greeks, and he became bilingual. His family had lived in a large house, surrounded by a white washed stucco wall capped with red tiles. The wall had been taller than Roger.

Roger's father had been transferred in 1960 to Kenya. A year later he was killed. Out in his car alone late at night to meet an agent, he ran into a roadblock manned by a band of African marauders. Desperate to escape, his father had spun his car, grabbing for a pistol in a shoulder holster. But a gunman had run to the side of the car and fired a submachine gun. Roger's father had died instantly.

Roger's idol, his father often had arranged activities of interest to a young boy, activities they could share. He had taught Roger to play baseball; they had fished in quick-moving trout streams in northern Greece and hunted ducks among the rushes along the southern coast of Thrace. Roger thrilled at each opportunity to carry his father's shotgun, when it wasn't loaded. They had had long conversations about right and wrong and values and morals. Roger had often thought those conversations were boring, but in later years he recognized how much they meant to him. He often remembered his father's exact words: "Roger, go apologize to your sister. Men don't speak that way to ladies," or, "Roger, tomorrow you go tell Vasili the real reason you didn't meet him after school. If your friends can't believe you, your words have no value, and then you have no value."

His father had taught him about patience. Once, while playing catch with a Greek friend behind his house in Athens, Roger accidentally threw the ball through the window of his father's study. When his father came out, Roger hurried to apologize, and told his father what had happened. His father gave a curt nod, as he always did when irritated, got in his car and left. He returned with a piece of glass and replaced the window.

Roger and his friend had continued playing catch, and not an hour later Roger threw the ball through the same window again. This time his father came out with a scowl, put both hands on Roger's head, turned it sharply to the right, and said, "Do you see that empty space there at the side of the house? That is where you will play catch." His father left in his car and shortly after returned with another piece of glass, and replaced the window again.

His father had chuckled often about the incident, but it didn't take much to make his father laugh. The slight wrinkles at the corners of his eyes showed that. His father was also close to his daughter, Mary Anne, and he tried to devote an equal amount of his time to her. Roger thought no one missed his father as much as he. His mother and sister didn't share that sentiment.

When his father was killed the agency moved the family back to the states, and following the custom, offered his mother a job. As the wife of an officer killed in the line of duty, she could work for CIA as long as she wished. The Agency took care of its own.

Full of resentment, feeling abandoned by his father, Roger rebelled during his early teens. His school friends were drug users and he shared their penchant to experiment. His hair grew almost to his shoulders, and he usually tied a red bandana around his head. His grades fell, and his mother failed in efforts to interest him in wholesome activities. Several of his father's former colleagues looked after the family, and they took Roger fishing, to baseball games to see the Baltimore Orioles and to Washington Redskins football games. Avoiding the urge to lecture him about his behavior, they told him stories of experiences with his father. They told him how his father stressed that though they were in the business of espionage, they had a moral obligation to maintain certain standards. They said his father believed that if CIA were to be successful in combating international communism and terrorism, its officers had to win the trust and confidence of those they wished to recruit to penetrate target organizations. Therefore, he said, each CIA officer had to establish a reputation of decency and integrity.

Those conversations increasingly took on more meaning, and by the time he reached his junior year in high school he had returned to some of the values his father had taught. He did well in his senior year and was accepted at Georgetown University—some of his father's friends who had graduated from Georgetown had put in a good word for him. He worked hard and graduated cum laude, with a degree in International Relations.

During his senior year he had decided to try to join CIA upon graduation, but his father's former colleagues discouraged the idea. They advised him not to join just because his father had been a CIA officer, and urged him to do something else for a few years, to gain experience before deciding on a career.

Roger had joined the Marines, was accepted in Officer Candidate School and commissioned a second lieutenant of infantry. As a platoon commander, and later as an executive officer of a rifle company, he spent almost two years in the Pacific. His battalion made training landings in Thailand, the Philippines, Okinawa, Japan and Korea. Roger loved the life of a Marine Corps officer; the camaraderie, the excitement, the roar of guns in firing exercises and the endless raucous discussions of possible combat opportunities over drinks at the club with his fellow officers. How else could they prove their courage, their leadership skills, their dedication to the men they commanded? Roger dreamed of becoming a general—why not commandant?

As the end of his tour approached, however, his thoughts had turned again to the CIA. He corresponded frequently with his father's friends, asking them for guidance. Without exception, they told him that after three years in the Marines he could make his own decision. Whatever he decided, they would support him.

Roger applied to join the CIA. Six months after his Marine Corps discharge, he received a letter from the CIA, inviting him for testing and evaluation.

He underwent an extensive period of evaluation: of psychological tests, including a long discussion about his father's death and the impact that had on his decision to become a CIA officer; of academic tests, including questions about philosophers who impressed him, and why, his favorite authors, and why. He was asked for his impressions of world religions, Marxism, Sino-Soviet relations. The economic future of Africa seemed important. After a polygraph examination, Roger entered a training program which, if completed satisfactorily, would lead to a commission as an officer in the Directorate of Operations, the "Clandestine Service."

The training program lasted almost a full year, and Roger's performance revealed him to be highly intelligent, innovative, quick to make decisions, controlled under pressure and eager to accept increasing responsibility. At the conclusion of his training Roger received a commission as an operations officer. He was a case officer, as his father had been, and it was the proudest moment of his life.

Privately, he wept because his father was not there to share it with him. His mother, though proud, was apprehensive.

At Georgetown University Roger had met a beautiful girl, Alexandra. She had been raised and educated in Switzerland, the daughter of American parents. Her father was an international banker. Tall, with deep blue eyes and long black hair that always seemed to be slightly wind blown, she was elegant and cultured. She spoke French and Italian in addition to slightly British-accented English. Roger had fallen deeply in love with her. A vivacious and witty young woman, they shared many laughs, and each enjoyed the other's company. She had flown to Hawaii three times to meet Roger when he was in the Marines. Since his return from the Marines, they had become inseparable until he began the year of training—most of it outside of Washington.

Not permitted to tell anyone of his CIA employment, he had lied to her about that year. He had been assigned the official cover of a Department of State Foreign Service officer, and the cover story he had to tell her was that he would be in Monterrey, California, studying diplomatic, military convergence in the Third World, and the application of force in international crises. With difficulty he fought off her insistence that she fly to California at least once a month to see him. During his training only a few hours outside of Washington, he was able to see her on the average of two weekends a month.

A week after his commissioning, and his assignment to an operational branch at CIA headquarters, he had invited Alexandra to the most elegant restaurant he could find in Washington and proposed to her over dinner. Her response was, "Of course I'll marry you, you ninny. I've known that since before you joined the Marines." Then came the hard part. He told her he was a CIA officer and had lied about where he'd been the last year. Her eyes filled with tears. "I thought," she said, haltingly, lowering her eyes, "that we shared everything. A whole year?" She was silent for a few moments, and then said, "I want to think about this, I'll tell you tomorrow. I worry about starting a marriage with a lie."

"I couldn't tell you," Roger said. "I'm a CIA officer, and we cannot admit that openly. Every officer in the Clandestine Service has an officially assigned cover under which he lives. For me to be assigned overseas without my past being backstopped by an official cover could be very dangerous for me—and for you as my wife. Please understand."

Alexandra said nothing, but the evening was ruined. She was silent in the car returning to her apartment, but as she left the car, she said, "Meet me in front of the Lincoln Memorial tomorrow at noon. It's Sunday, and I presume the CIA will give you the day off."

Roger couldn't sleep. He wanted desperately for Alexandra to be his wife, and after his third scotch, at two in the morning, he decided that if Alexandra refused to marry him because of the CIA, he would resign.

In the morning he couldn't eat, and sat looking through his kitchen window, drinking coffee and lighting one cigarette off the other. Three times the phone rang. He thought it surely was his mother, and didn't answer.

He arrived at the memorial an hour early. Shortly before noon he saw Alexandra approaching from around the reflecting pool. When she saw him her pace quickened, and as she neared she broke into a run. He reached to embrace her, but she threw her right arm around his neck, punched him hard in the mid-section with her left, and said, "I'd love to be the wife of a spy. Let's get married."

They were married a month later, but faced a difficult time trying to live as a married couple.

After six months, learning how a headquarters branch functioned to support an overseas station, Roger was assigned to Cyprus, with the cover title of second secretary in the political section of the embassy.

It seemed a perfect post for him and his new bride. But the island's beauty, lush, verdant mountains and quaint villages, surrounded by the sparkling eastern Mediterranean Sea, one of the ancient centers of worship of Aphrodite, the Greek goddess of love, masked an undercurrent of ethnic hatred and distrust.

Although Greek Cypriots marveled at Roger's Athenian-accented Greek, he struggled with the Cypriot dialect, particularly those vestiges of ancient Ionian Greek spoken in the area of Paphos at the island's western end. He took lessons to learn the Greek Cypriot dialects and regional idiomatic expressions. The northern coast, heavily populated by Turkish Cypriots, was rocky and rugged, and in the deep clear blue waters the snorkeling was superb. Roger taught Alexandra to snorkel, and although panicking at her first sight of the water's depth, with much cajoling and encouragement she quickly became an avid fan. They spent many weekends swimming on the north coast and dining at small outdoor tavernas around the quaint harbor of Kyrenia.

On the south coast, outside the cities of Famagusta and Larnaca, the wide sandy beaches often hosted embassy beach parties. But not long after their arrival in Cyprus, the political situation began to deteriorate. The mainland Greek government supported a coup to overthrow Cypriot president, Archbishop Makarios, and when a known anti-Turk, a Greek Cypriot gunman, was installed as president by the Greek government, the Turkish army invaded to protect the large Turkish minority. Because of widespread fighting, American families and all non-essential embassy personnel were evacuated. Alexandra, who was pregnant, chose to go to Athens.

The letter Roger wrote her every day helped assuage his longing, but he was relieved that she was off the island and out of danger.

His own life suddenly became more dangerous. Initially assigned to work on the local Soviet target—to recruit a KGB officer or a Soviet diplomat—when community fighting erupted, all officers of the CIA station immediately turned their attention to cover the political crisis. Faced with the imminent threat that Greece and Turkey, both members of NATO, might go to war, the CIA moved rapidly to acquire new information sources and influence in both the Greek Cypriot and the Turkish Cypriot communities.

Roger's new orders directed him toward recruitment of penetration agents in the small but deadly Greek Cypriot terrorist groups, one of which would soon shoot and kill the American ambassador. Meeting a member of a terrorist group at two in the morning in a CIA safehouse, with fighting raging outside, was not, Roger discovered, for the faint of heart. Station officers worked seven days a week and spent most nights meeting agents. The pace and stress were grinding.

Roger, able to go to Athens to see Alexandra for a couple of days about once every six weeks; struggled at the end of each visit with the necessity to return to Cyprus. But his short visits restored his stamina and willingness to return to his life of daily apprehension. Their first child, a daughter, was born. They named her Debra. But Roger couldn't leave Cyprus, and did not see his daughter until she was nine weeks old.

After eighteen months of separation from Alexandra, Roger received orders to take four weeks of leave and then report to headquarters to prepare for an assignment to Beirut. The night before his departure from Cyprus, his station colleagues did their best to ensure that Roger's arrival in Athens and his reunion with his wife would be as inauspicious as an all night drinking party could make it. When he arrived in Athens to collect his wife and daughter, Alexandra was so relieved that he was out of Cyprus for good that she quickly forgave him his condition.

In Athens they bought a new car and spent almost four weeks driving through Europe; up the east coast of Italy to the lake country, crossing into Switzerland and then to Germany. They drove up the Rhine River to Cologne. From a language guide they memorized how to ask in German for a double room with bath and crib, or how to order a meal, but they could never understand the response. They laughed self-consciously about their inability to speak German, but were saved much embarrassment by German graciousness and the many who spoke excellent English or French. From Cologne they turned west to Brussels, and then spent three days in Paris, mostly sitting at small outdoor cafes, people-watching, sipping campari and sodas, and gently rocking Debra in her folding stroller. From Paris they went to Le Havre and boarded a ship for a five-day sail to New York.

Alexandra expected this to be a trip of a lifetime, but Roger had changed. He was unable to sleep well. The slightest noise; the backfire of a car, the slamming of a door or even the sliding of a chair at an outdoor café startled him. At night in bed, if she moved or coughed, he awakened immediately. He couldn't relax.

When Roger checked into headquarters, they received devastating news. A civil war had erupted in Lebanon, and the State Department and the CIA had decided to evacuate all embassy families in Beirut to Athens. Though Alexandra and their daughter could go to Athens, Roger was ordered to Beirut alone.

Beautiful Beirut hugged the shore of the eastern Mediterranean; the financial center of the Middle East, a sophisticated, elegant, and cosmopolitan city. Fresh oysters were flown in every day from Paris. The polyglot population was being ripped apart by civil war: Christian against Muslim, Christian against Christian, Muslim against Muslim. The view from the plane approaching the city, the azure sea with snow-capped mountains in the background, obscured the bombed-out buildings, deserted neighborhoods, rubble in the streets, families torn apart, and thousands of refugees—the legacy of bitter urban warfare.

Roger joined Jack Kelly and three other officers in the dangerous task of penetrating Palestinian terrorist groups. American officials were special targets of terrorist organizations, and CIA officers were at the top of their lists. Self-preservation motivated the case officers to be aggressive in their efforts to neutralize these groups. The CIA station had penetration agents in most of the organizations and case officers met those agents once or twice weekly, always at night and clandestinely. To obtain information on the plans and intentions of the terrorist organizations was vital. But equally important was the collection of assessment data on members of those organizations who might be vulnerable to CIA recruitment. Planning how to recruit a member of a terrorist organization was always done with alacrity, but the devil was in the details.

After carefully debriefing several agents who knew a regional director of the Popular Front for the Liberation of Palestine—the PFLP—a particularly virulent and aggressive terrorist group, the station made a decision. They had collected enough assessment data to consider him a recruitment target. They would go after him.

The station knew that the target, with the *nom de guerre* of Abu Jihad, held a degree in architecture from a local university, and discovered that one of his former professors had left Beirut to live in Brussels, Belgium. They knew that Abu Jihad was unemployed and worried about supporting his wife and son. And he had been heard to say that he understood the need to use violence to focus world attention on the plight of the Palestinian people under Israeli occupation. But he abhorred it.

The station printed stationery with the letterhead of a Belgian construction company involved in projects worldwide. They then wrote Abu Jihad a letter which said that upon the recommendation of his former professor who lived in Belgium, the company wished to invite Abu Jihad to an employment interview at a given hour and date at one of the large Beirut hotels.

Abu Jihad arrived for the interview where he met a station case officer in disguise, posing as a recruiter for the Belgian company. Over a series of meetings, the ostensible Belgian paid Abu Jihad for sample architectural drawings. CIA headquarters evaluated the drawings and passed critical comments back to Abu Jihad as if they had come from the Belgian company. The case officer then gave Abu Jihad assignments to draw a passenger processing building at a United Arab Emirates airport, which had tight security requirements, and a new wing to a Belgian Consulate in East Africa. The case officer paid Abu Jihad several thousand dollars for his drawings. Abu Jihad expressed great delight in this new relationship and repeatedly affirmed his appreciation for the opportunity the case officer had given him.

The case officer then introduced Abu Jihad to another case officer, also in disguise, posing as an American who worked for a Belgian security company that had a contract to provide security for all the Belgian construction company's projects. After several meetings, during which the American discussed in detail the security aspects of Abu Jihad's drawings of the United Emirates airport and the Belgian consulate addition, the American offered Abu Jihad a job as a consultant to his company at a monthly salary three times that which the first case officer had paid him for his drawings. Abu Jihad was snared. The words "CIA," "PFLP" or "terrorism" never came up. No one will ever know when Abu Jihad recognized his transition from consultant to spy, but the money was too good and the future too bright—if he didn't get caught—to make an issue of it. He became a highly productive penetration of the PFLP.

The station moved quickly to change the venue of their meetings with Abu Jihad from a hotel to a safehouse and then, after the relationship was solid, changed the meetings to car pick-ups late at night.

The political situation and the spreading violence eventually made it too dangerous for case officers to meet their Palestinian agents alone in safehouses. The case officers feared that an agent might be caught and confess, and then lead an assassination or kidnap team to the next safehouse meeting, leaving the case officer with no way to escape. Case officers began picking up their agents in cars at night from darkened street corners, and conducting the meetings while driving on back streets or parked in alleys. To protect their fellow officers, to ensure that they were not under surveillance and to cover them should they run into a roadblock, two case officers always followed in a car behind the officer making the pick-up. In the tail car the officers were heavily armed, always with hand guns, and either a shotgun or a submachine gun and tear gas grenades. They did this night after night, sometimes twice a night, and often seven nights a week. The bond between case officers became the most important in their lives. They shared apartments, ate together, drank together and spent almost all their free time together. They joked that the title, "Band of Brothers," originated with them. But the lifestyle and the ever-present danger took its toll.

One case officer suffered a nervous breakdown and was evacuated. One was killed when he turned his car ignition key and a bomb exploded. And one night, after covering an agent pick-up, Roger and Jack Kelly drove into a Muslim area of Beirut, looking for the address of a Palestinian who they had decided might be a good candidate for recruitment, if they could gain access to him. Roger, who was driving, had turned into a particularly dark street when gunfire erupted. The firing between two rival groups had caught them in the middle. Shots blew out the windshield, and Jack was driven against the seat. With a low moan he slumped forward, blood flowing onto the dashboard and the floor. Roger, in desperation, backed out of the block at full speed, hitting two parked cars, swung the car around and drove frantically to the hospital of the American University of Beirut, where Jack was rushed to surgery.

An hour or so later a Lebanese surgeon told Roger that Jack had been shot in the left shoulder. The shoulder was broken, but the shot had not damaged his lung or his heart. He was stable, was being given transfusions, and would survive.

Two days later Jack had been evacuated by a helicopter from a United States aircraft carrier stationed somewhere between Lebanon and Cyprus and flown to Frankfurt, Germany, and then to Washington.

Roger had missed Jack a great deal, and he became morose and fatalistic. He thought it likely that the remaining two, of the original five case officers, would not leave Beirut alive. He began to drink heavily and his behavior became impulsive and irresponsible. Newly arrived case officer replacements still volunteered to ride with him at night because they valued his experience on the street, but they were concerned about what he might do. He kept a bottle in his operational car, and frequently drank when covering an agent pick-up. He also kept a pistol in his lap, a round in the chamber and the safety off. They worried that he might shoot one of them by accident or someone else without cause. His reporting from his own agent meetings became sloppy and incomplete, and while he never appeared drunk, he arrived at the office some mornings smelling of alcohol and obviously hung over.

Although the station had sent no official report to headquarters about his behavior, word got back and a cable arrived, ordering Roger home. A decision had been made to assign him to an operational branch in the Soviet Division in headquarters for two years and to observe his behavior and performance. Senior headquarters officers decided he should be reunited with his wife and daughter and spend some quiet time with them.

When he reported to the branch he had a slight facial twitch, he was smoking three packs of cigarettes a day and his hands displayed a slight tremor. The chief of the branch thought he was on the edge.

But it was a good time for Roger and Alexandra. His daughter fascinated him, and for the first time he could spend long hours with her. He loved taking her to the zoo and holding her hand as she squealed and giggled at what she saw. When she put her arms around his neck and kissed him good night, his voice often cracked as he told her, "Sweet dreams."

Roger had performed well at the branch. He quickly adapted to life at headquarters and gained a reputation as an excellent briefer. He wrote well and quickly, and his operational judgment was sound. Closely observed at dinner and cocktail parties, he gained a reputation as a witty raconteur and a welcome addition to any social gathering. Alexandra became pregnant again.

Near the end of a two-year assignment at headquarters, Roger requested another overseas assignment, and his division senior officers concurred. He was ready to go again. At one of the frequent Washington cocktail parties his division chief asked Alexandra what kind of posting she and Roger wanted, and she said, "We don't really care where, but please send us somewhere where we can live together and Roger's life will not be in danger. We've been overseas over four years, and except for a few months in Cyprus; we've not been able to live together. We've always been separated."

The following summer Roger had been assigned to Kavalla, a modest tobacco and fishing town on the Aegean Sea in northeastern Greece. His orders were to represent the CIA at an interrogation center run jointly by the CIA and the Greek Intelligence Service, "KYP," to process Bulgarian refugees who escaped across the border into Greece. He also had to supervise a CIA interrogator at the center, and from the refugee flow to recruit and train cross-border agents for dispatch back to Bulgaria, when and if the need arose. His assignment included mounting recruitment operations against the Greek Communist Party, the "KKE." Kavalla was the birthplace of the KKE and was still a center of communist activities. Specifically, CIA wanted to know how the Soviet Communist Party financed the KKE.

It sounded dull to Roger, but Alexandra was ecstatic. She had no idea what Roger's responsibilities were, but they were living together as a family in a spacious home on a hill overlooking the town and the Aegean. The view from their bedroom balcony was breathtaking, a town of whitewashed buildings with red tiled roofs, and a snug harbor overflowing with small fishing boats. CIA was pleased to have a Greek-speaking officer in northern Greece, and satisfied that Roger needed a tour in a place politically stable.

Located some forty miles south of the Bulgarian border, close by ruins of the ancient Macedonian city of Phillipi, Kavalla offered a life style far different from the turmoil and strife Roger left behind in Cyprus and Beirut. Small outdoor tavernas ringing the harbor nightly served grilled fish, squid, octopus, dolmades with avgolemono sauce and young lamb cooked over charcoal. In the evenings the whole town smelled of charcoal and roasting meat. White sand beaches with clear, calm waters drew them like magnets on the weekends.

Alexandra gave birth to their second child: a daughter, Valerie. Roger was content as never before.

But duty called again, and at the end of his third year in Kavalla, the station moved Roger and his family to Athens, where he worked in liaison with KYP. In Athens he contacted many of his childhood friends, and he and Alexandra shared their social life among Roger's many Greek friends and station colleagues. Alexandra learned enough Greek to shop and to be polite at social gatherings, and she would have been satisfied to spend the rest of her life in Greece. But after two years, Roger decided that five years in Greece was enough. He had a career to pursue, and he asked to be transferred.

Within a few months Roger received orders to report to CIA headquarters, where he again reported to the Soviet Division. He and Alexandra bought their first home and lived a quiet but busy life in the Virginia suburbs; and time passed quickly. There, Alexandra and Jack Kelly's wife, Barbara, became fast friends, sharing their chagrin about how much whiskey their husbands drank when together.

At the end of his tour in headquarters, Roger was appointed deputy chief of the station in Vienna, Austria, and assigned to ten months of language training. In Vienna they found a large, elegant apartment in the old city with separate bedrooms for the girls and quarters for a maid. Roger worked long hours, but they spent most of the winter weekends skiing. Alexandra tried to teach him to ski—a payback for having had to learn to snorkel in Cyprus. Alexander had skied throughout her childhood in Switzerland. She was a superb skier. Roger was mediocre at best and actually had no great affection for the sport. He went along because of Alexandra.

Roger didn't like his job in Vienna. The chief of station made all the important operational decisions, leaving Roger to do all the things the chief didn't want to do: overlook the finances, prepare personnel reports, edit intelligence reports and conduct liaison with the Austrian intelligence service. He longed to be on the street with the case officers.

After three years in Vienna, with orders designating him as chief of station, Rome, he and Alexandra returned to Washington. There Roger studied Italian for eight months. Alexandra was a great help, because her Italian was excellent, but critical of what she called his Greek accent.

Once in Rome, they fell in love with the city and the warm, noisy, bustling Italians, and devoted as much time as possible traveling throughout the country. They took their evening *passegiata* with their neighbors, nodding and greeting each other as they strolled around their neighborhood square.

Again, Alexandra thought she could spend the rest of her life there. But after three years in Rome, CIA headquarters once more interrupted her reverie, ordering Roger to Washington to become deputy chief of the European Division. Though reluctant to leave Rome, he couldn't afford to turn down the assignment and the promotion that went with it. After one year as the deputy, Roger became the chief of the division.

Caught up in the Washington bureaucracy, Jack Kelly and Beirut seemed long in the past. But Roger had thought often of their experiences, and he was anxious to see Jack again. Roger knew that Jack, having just returned as chief of station,

Bosnia, would have much to say about U.S. involvement there. Roger would listen with interest, but it was enough for him that Jack had left Bosnia safely.

Chapter 2

▼

John Kelly entered Roger's office the next morning at ten-fifteen. The tall slender man, graying at the temples, extended his hand with a broad grin. Roger pushed it aside; they both laughed and embraced.

"Roger, its good to see you. How've you been?"

"Great, Jack, and its good to see you. How was Bosnia? When did you leave there?"

"I left there about six weeks ago, but I took a month home leave and checked in about two weeks ago. I called you as soon as I got here, but you were on a trip to London."

Jack sat on the couch. Square jawed, with deep-set blue eyes and an aristocratic look; he crossed long legs. Roger took a chair across the coffee table, facing him.

"I know, Alexandra told me, but I was away longer than I planned. I had to go to Paris and Bonn and just got home two days ago. Barbara was so excited that you were coming home. I tried to tell her that you would be your same old grouchy self."

"Yeah, she told me you said that. You're a helluva friend. But I'll tell you, buddy, eighteen months is a long time to be separated. Why am I telling you that? Hell, you know, we've both done that before. It was easier for me because I was damned busy. There wasn't much time to reflect on anything except what was going on around us."

"Did you do any good in Bosnia?"

"Who knows,? It was a tough tour, but we ran some very good operations."

Jack told of the economic misery of Bosnia and the wrenching hate and desire for revenge. He thought it would take many years before any semblance of normalcy returned to the area.

"But you know,' he continued, "the young case officers thrive on it. They're like you and I were in Beirut. They work eighteen-hour days, seven days a week. You can't make them take any time off."

"That shows you provided good leadership. You motivated them," Roger said.

"Oh, for God's sake Roger, we've been at this long enough to know how to motivate case officers: just let them do their thing, and stay out of the way. All I had to do was stay awake twenty hours a day. I guess they thought that if the old man can stay awake they'd better stay busy. But more important than that, there's talk in the halls that you're thinking about retiring. Is that true?"

"No, not yet. I want one more tour. I've asked for Paris next summer. If that works out, I'd like to stay there three years and then retire. But I'd need some language training. My French is rusty. How about you? How do you like the CI staff? I never knew counterintelligence was your bag."

"It's not, you know I have no CI background, but it's going to be okay. You know, Roger, if you have to be at headquarters, it's better to spend your time looking at operational files than dealing with administrative and budgetary matters as you do in this job."

"You're right, I don't have much time to concentrate on operations. I presume that's why they assign a chief of operations to your staff," Roger said, shrugging.

"I guess. Have you had time to look at the file I sent you yesterday?" Jack asked.

"I read the file."

"Do you remember the case? His name was Kolev."

"You know Jack, there've been so many operations, lots of agents. Do you realize that we've been in this business twenty-four years? At first I had no recollection, but as I went through the file it began to come back. I remember now that it was a sad case, but very low-level. That was so long ago what possible significance could the case have now? Why would the CI staff care about this?"

"Well, we have word of Mister Ivan Kolev. He is in Sofia and he's serving a life sentence for committing espionage on behalf of CIA."

"You're kidding."

"No. At least that's what the Bulgarians have told us," Jack replied, reaching for a pack of cigarettes. He offered one to Roger, who shook his head. Jack put the cigarettes on the coffee table.

"What are we supposed to do about it now?" Roger asked.

"I'm not sure. But I'll give you some background. As you know, Roger, since the evil empire fell apart we've established liaison relations with almost all of the services of the former Warsaw Pact countries. So now we and the Bulgarians talk. The Bulgarian government is reviewing all cases of people imprisoned under the Communist government for political crimes. This case, Kolev, is under review as we speak. Kolev escaped into Greece in 1983. He claims he escaped solely to find a better life in the West and said he wanted to resettle in some Western country and find a decent job. He maintains that the Greeks took him to a place where both Greeks and Americans interrogated him, and told him that if he told the truth he would be processed as a refugee and helped to resettle."

Roger leaned back, loosened his tie and unbuttoned the top button of his shirt. He rose, walked to his desk and from a silver thermos poured two cups of coffee and returned to his chair, placing a cup in front of Jack.

"That's true," he said. "I'm sure I've told you about how we worked that, but I'll tell you again."

Roger explained that CIA had run a joint interrogation center with the Greek service, just outside Kavalla, that processed about one hundred Bulgarian refugees a year. The Greeks and CIA both interrogated each refugee for positive intelligence, and if it was determined that they were clean, not on a mission for the Bulgarians, the refugees were sent to a camp for resettlement. About five percent of the refugees were caught as Bulgarian agents. Those people were subjected to a hostile interrogation, and when they broke and confessed, they were turned over to the Greeks, who sent them to Salonika and subjected them to a military court martial. Most of those were hanged.

"Weren't most of those rather low-level agents?" Jack asked.

"Many were, but for example, the mission of one of them was to resettle in Chicago and in the event of hostilities to poison the Chicago waterworks. Some of them were Bulgarian army officers under cover, and some were coerced by the Bulgarian service to undertake a mission. We let those go."

"I understand," Jack said, "but Kolev maintains that when his interrogation was completed—and he was not a Bulgarian agent—the Americans told him that he could not proceed through refugee channels until he earned the right to settle in the West, and then coerced to become a cross-border agent. You sent him on a mission against his will."

"He's not telling the truth. He wasn't coerced. You know as well as I that you can't coerce someone to undertake a mission like that with any confidence that he'll be loyal to you. The truth is that at the time we recruited him we had about twelve refugees in the interrogation center. We didn't run many agents into Bulgaria in those days. The overhead coverage made that unnecessary. But we always tried to keep one trained and on hand in the event something came up that required some human activity inside Bulgaria that our Sofia station couldn't handle for one reason or another. And we didn't have one at that time. Of the twelve refugees, we considered three to be possible candidates. We approached all three of them, but only Kolev accepted. Our standard offer was five thousand dollars for one mission and the promise that when they returned we would see that they were taken into the U.S. Army for three years. If they completed three years of honorable service, we would sponsor a private bill in Congress to grant them U.S. citizenship. It was not a bad offer for someone with a little adventure in his soul."

"Roger, Kolev is saying that he went on the mission for us, but since he had been sent against his will, he turned himself in. He maintains that the Bulgarian service then recruited him as a double agent and dispatched him back to us to penetrate our cross-border program being run out of Kavalla."

"That's true. Where'd you get all of this?" Roger asked.

"Well, the Bulgarians passed it to the station and asked if we could help them with the truth about Kolev's involvement. Kolev maintains that he succeeded in his mission for the Bulgarian service and did, in fact, penetrate our program, gained our confidence, and we, unaware of his loyalty to the Bulgarian service, sent him on a second mission."

"Jack, you know from the file that he didn't penetrate our program. We broke him."

"I know, but then why is Kolev claiming he did. What does that imply?" Jack propped both feet on the coffee table.

"Simple, I think, it implies that he didn't tell the Bulgarian service that we broke him when he returned from the first mission," Roger said. "And take your feet off my table!"

Jack removed his feet. They both laughed.

"Then why is he in prison?" Jack asked.

"I think I know. But it's not in the file."

"I'm glad you said that, Roger, because your reporting wasn't very good on this case. The last part of the file, as you saw, says only that he confessed to being doubled by the Bulgarians while on his first mission. And it also says simply that since the Greeks wanted you to get rid of him, you sent him back to Bulgaria on a bogus mission; one from which you were satisfied he would not return to Greece. The file does say that there is a CI addendum containing the details of his confession. But for some reason that was sent to archives separately. I haven't recovered it yet, because I presumed it might not be relevant, and I knew you'd brief me on it.

"You know, I may have to go out to Bulgaria to discuss this case with them," Jack continued. "It depends on what we decide here. So, tell me how you broke him, and what you did to ensure he wouldn't return to Greece."

"Well," Roger said, "we liked this kid. He wasn't well-educated, but he was bright. He simply got in over his head. He had spunk but, in retrospect, he shouldn't have been involved."

"Who is we? The file provides only the pseudonym of the guy who worked with you on this," Jack said. "I'd hate to do a CI review of all your operations, Roger, because you've always told headquarters as little as possible about what you were doing."

"Jack, why should I report to headquarters what they already know? Headquarters knew whom they assigned to Kavalla. In any case, his name was John Nemchov. That wasn't his real name, because we had had his name changed legally. He was a former Bulgarian army officer, the son of a general, and a graduate of the military academy. He was a captain when his father died, and after his father died John went through a nasty divorce. His wife was the daughter of a member of the Central Committee of the Communist Party. When John divorced his wife, her father made certain that his life was hell, and they kicked him out of the army. He had difficulty finding a job, but finally landed one as a truck driver. When his ex-father-in-law found out, he had him fired. He then got a job at a lumber camp, cutting trees, but the same thing happened. So he escaped to Turkey. We picked him up and sent him back on a mission. He did such a good job, and he was so capable, that we hired him as a contract agent and sent him back here for testing and training. Obviously, as a contract agent, he was never allowed in the headquarters' building, but we trained him as an interrogator and sent him to Kavalla as our interrogator at the center. He also helped out with the training of cross-border agents, and he was good at it. He was also a superb interrogator."

"Where is he now?"

"The poor guy died of a heart attack two years ago," Roger said, shaking his head. "He was a good guy. Anyway, we trained Kolev well, as I recall, and by the time we sent him in he was good with a map and compass, a good photographer and in good physical condition. He was only fair with a weapon, but that wasn't important anyway, because we gave them weapons training only as a morale booster, to give them confidence. We knew that if they ran into a Bulgarian border guard patrol, they weren't going to win any fire fights armed only with a handgun. He took to the training well and was diligent in every training assignment we gave him.

"But we discovered one thing that turned out to be significant. We always had a safehouse keeper with Kolev on training exercises and, in fact, he was never allowed out without the safehouse keeper. The safehouse keeper was a guy named Petros, I believe, a tough former Greek guerilla-fighter. Petros reported to us that Kolev had an extraordinary fear of lightning. Several times when Petros and Kolev were out on hiking exercises, they were caught in thunderstorms, and Petros said Kolev would literally become frozen with fear. His whole body would tremble, and he'd become incoherent."

Roger recounted that the night John and he put Kolev across the border on his first mission, the area was struck by a severe thunderstorm not long after Kolev crossed. There was a great deal of lightning.

"John and I were worried about it, and it turned out we had good reason. The night he returned from the mission, John and I were relieved and genuinely happy that he was safe. At the border, we put him in the back of our jeep and started for the safehouse, which was just south of Kavalla. But before we reached the house, both John and I independently felt that something was wrong."

"Why?" Jack asked, returning his feet to the coffee table.

"That wasn't the first mission we'd put across the border. In all the other operations, the agents were so ecstatic to be back safely that the last thing they wanted to discuss was another mission. But almost the first thing out of this guy's mouth was to tell us that the mission was exciting, and that he'd like another one. He also didn't appear as haggard as he should have after a five-day mission.

"But John and I didn't reveal our concerns to each other immediately, because we had arranged a feast for him at the house. We had a whole baby goat cooked on a spit, and we had plenty of retsina wine and ouzo."

"That dreadful wine that tastes like turpentine?" Jack asked.

"The same. So, we had a great party that went on much too long."

"I can imagine, Roger. I've seen you in action before."

"I held my own," Roger said, chuckling. "We started questioning him the next day, and by that time John and I were suspicious of him."

"Why? Those casual observations you made in the jeep weren't alone serious enough to make you both suspicious," Jack said.

"No. You're right. We had other things. For example, during his training we sent him on a five-day exercise equal in difficulty to the mission we were planning for him. When he returned, we took a full-face photograph of him. He looked haggard and worn. When we arrived at the house that morning, we took another photograph, as we always did. In the second he didn't look as tired, and John and I agreed that he could not have traveled the distance and through the terrain the mission required and appear so fresh. The difference was striking. Also we examined his shoes. They were worn, but not evenly, and as much as they should have been. We examined the photographs he took. They were taken at the place we sent him, but a column of military vehicles blocked the view of the site. We considered that was possibly a coincidence, and we would have accepted it if everything else sounded right. So we wondered."

Roger picked up the pack of cigarettes from the coffee table and gave one to Jack and took one himself. He lit them both.

"Anyway," Roger continued, "we were in that frame of mind when we started his debriefing the next day. We had trained him using a one-to-fifty-thousand scale map and we debriefed him from a one-to-twenty-five-thousand scale map. Much more detail. His first problem was in describing where he arrived at the Mesta River. We plotted his compass heading on the map, so we knew exactly where he had arrived at the river. When he told us that he arrived there, we asked what he saw to his right. He said he saw a factory. He was right: there was a factory to his right, but our map showed that between his position and the factory a small promontory jutted a few dozen meters into the river and it was twenty-five meters in elevation. He couldn't have seen the factory from where he was. The one-to-fifty-thousand scale map didn't show that detail. Farther on, he had made a notation in his notebook showing that he shot an azimuth at the eastern-most mountain peak where two peaks of similar elevation stood side by side. We asked him what the terrain was like under his feet when he took the compass reading. He thought for a moment, and said, 'The ground was level.' It couldn't have been. Tracking the kilometers he was covering on foot per hour by reading his notations, and his recorded compass sightings, he would've been on the steep western slope of a three-thousand-foot mountain. If the ground were level when he shot the azimuth, he obviously took the reading from a plain north of that position, and he couldn't have walked that far in that time. We went through his trek in such detail for two days."

Roger said that he and John had taken the morning of the third day to review all of Kolev's statements, and that they collated all his errors in fact. Then they went to the house to confront him.

"When we all sat down at the table, we told him he was lying to us and we were going to stay there until we got to the bottom of it. He was shocked. We had not let on to him until then that we had any doubts. He, of course, protested. He swore on everything he could possibly think of that he had told us the absolute truth. We then took him through his route on our map and pointed out to him every mistake he had made. We counted nineteen. We told him we knew he had traveled much of the route in a vehicle and we pointed out to him on the map which stretches he had walked, and which he had been driven.

"When we finished, he fell silent. He refused to respond to our questions. We told him we knew something happened to him on the mission he had not told us about, and we reminded him of the Greek law covering espionage on behalf of a foreign government, and, you know, the consequences of turning him over to the Greeks. We also told him that from that moment on we considered him hostile and would deal with him accordingly. We made him stand, and told him he would continue standing until he told us the truth."

"You didn't get physical with him, did you?" Jack put his cigarette out.

"No. We didn't have to," Roger answered. "For example, we showed him the shoes he wore on the mission and how they were worn differently from those he wore on the training exercises before his mission. We told him we didn't know how they became worn that way, but we knew it wasn't from walking on his mission.

"We then went through the notations he had made in his notebook. We showed him how all the entries were on an even line and orderly in their sequence, and then showed him the notebook he used during his training exercises. Many of those entries were on slanting or wavy lines, some scrunched together, and others scrawled unevenly across the page. We told him his training notebook entries appeared that way because he was leaning against a tree, writing with his notebook balanced on his knee, or he was kneeling, covered by his jacket to hide his light. Obviously, the way those entries were made depended on his position when he wrote them. The entries in his mission notebook, we told him, appeared to us to have been written all at the same time and in the same position, as if he were sitting at a desk. We asked, 'If a handwriting expert examined the entries in your notebook, would he confirm our suspicions?' He said nothing. So we also told him that when we issued him his weapon we made sure there were only two sets of fingerprints on it—his and mine. Now his weapon revealed prints from at least four other people. We asked, 'How did they get there?' We were lying to him about the fingerprints. We had no fingerprint capability in Kavalla, but at that point we knew he had been in the hands of the Bulgarians, so someone else would have touched the weapon.

"With that, he buried his head in his hands and crumbled slowly to his knees. He began sobbing. I think he thought he was a dead man. John pulled his hands away from his face and showed him the two close-up photographs, one from the training exercise, and the one following the mission, and said, 'Ivan, my boy, explain to us the difference between these two photographs.'

"Kolev asked, between sobs, 'May I get up? I'll tell you everything.'

"And he did. He started talking, and he told us an interesting story."

Chapter 3

"John helped him up and put him in the chair. We gave him a cigarette, poured him a little brandy and waited until he pulled himself together. That took quite a while, because he was damned upset."

Jack pulled out a small notebook and made notes.

"I remember his hands were shaking so badly he had trouble putting the cigarette in his mouth," Roger said.

"He told us of a terrible thunderstorm just after we put him across the border. He was less than half a kilometer inside. Lightening struck nearby, terrifying him, and during a second flash, he saw in the distance a building with a Bulgarian flag. He ran to that building. It was a border guard post, and he gave himself up. He said that under no circumstances could he have carried on in that weather because he was afraid to move, and afraid to stay where he was.

"As you said, Jack, details of his confession aren't relevant now, but let me tell you a little about it very quickly—you'll like this: A colonel, obviously from the DS, picked him up the next morning and took him to Sofia."

"The DS, is that what they called the service?" Jack asked.

"Yeah, but they've changed the name now. Anyway, the colonel was good. He obviously had realized he had a scared and vulnerable kid on his hands, one who represented a golden opportunity to recruit and send back to penetrate our cross-border activities. So he treated Kolev as if he were his uncle. In two days he recruited him, and we were convinced he recruited him ideologically, without bribes or threats. And he motivated Kolev to return to us as a dedicated double agent under control of the DS. I believe if we hadn't broken him he'd still be working for them."

After recruiting Kolev, Roger explained, the colonel had driven and walked with Kolev through the route of his mission. He helped him record compass readings along the route, gave him contract instructions to use if he came back to Bulgaria on another mission, and he gave him contract instructions to use if he were settled in the West. He also arranged for a military convoy to be parked in front of the site Kolev had to photograph, and before he put him back across the border, made him write the notations in his notebook. And he had his driver rub Kolev's shoes on a rock to make them look worn. The colonel had done a good job and got a lot accomplished in five days," Roger said.

"Yeah, but it wasn't good enough, Roger. So what happened then? What did you do with him?" Jack asked.

"Then we had one helluva problem. We locked Kolev up and, of course, reported to the Greeks that we had a confessed double agent on our hands. We had kept them informed about the case from the time we recruited him, and they had helped us put him across the border and retrieve him. Well, the Greeks immediately demanded that we turn Kolev over to them for court martial. They would have executed him. I didn't blame them. They had a confessed Bulgarian spy on their soil, and that's what their law demanded.

"But we weren't going to let that happen. John and I felt sorry for Kolev. He was a simple guy and he started out looking only for a better life. If not for a morbid fear of lightening he would have come back from the mission, gone into the Army and probably lived a reasonably comfortable and secure life. Even if he had returned from the mission and told us what had happened to him, we probably would still have helped him resettle somewhere in the West. Once in the colonel's hands, however, he was out of his depth. He had to accept the colonel's recruitment pitch, but he shouldn't have tried to carry it out. When he decided to do that, he no longer controlled his destiny.

"We had kept Kolev in the interrogation center for almost five months. Our station in Athens had an ongoing row with KYP, and the minister of interior, and our relations with the local KYP office were getting progressively worse. Finally, the Greeks told us to get Kolev out of the country, or they were going to take him under their jurisdiction whether we approved or not. They, of course, could have done that anytime they wanted."

"Wait a minute, Roger," Jack interrupted. "I want to make a couple of notes." He started writing.

Roger stood and walked to the wall of windows. It was raining again. He wondered if he had done the right thing in the Kolev case. He remembered he had considered suggesting to headquarters that they take Kolev to the states, have him activate the contact instructions the colonel had given him, and wait and see who contacted Kolev. It would probably have been some sleeper agent the Bulgarians had in the states, and perhaps the CIA could have doubled him or at least have the FBI arrest him. But then, Roger had reasoned, the agency would have been stuck with Kolev and his welfare for the rest of the man's life.

"Roger, you still with us?" Jack said, amused that Roger suddenly seemed to have drifted off. "So what happened next?"

Roger returned to his chair. "Well, so we finally decided to send him back to Bulgaria. But we didn't want to risk having the Bulgarians dispatch him to some other Western country with a new identity. He was, you know, a fully recruited DS agent, and if they trusted him, they would have no reason not to use him in some other operation. To prevent that, we decided to neutralize him—send him back but introduce distrust into his relationship with the DS, something to prevent the DS from fully establishing his bona fides."

"If he's serving a life sentence for espionage, you certainly succeeded. How'd you do it?"

"We had devised a bogus mission for him. We knew from several refugee interrogations that a factory just south of Ruse made maps of Greece and Turkey that the Soviets used in their missile targeting. We also knew the director of the factory was named Atanasov, or something like that. I forget his first name. He was known to be an ardent Communist, and we had information he was an informant for the local security office. For the mission we armed Kolev with false Bulgarian identification, and once over the border he had to take public transportation to the factory. We told him Atanasov would expect him, and that Atanasov would give him sets of those maps to bring back to Greece."

"Had we ever had any contact with this man, Atanasov?" Jack asked.

"Oh, heavens, no. Atanasov had never heard of us."

"You didn't do him any favors, did you?" Jack said, grimacing.

"No. And in those days we didn't care. Why not get rid of him too?"

"Did you ever hear what happened to him?"

"No. But if Kolev is serving life in prison, Atanasov might be in the next cell," Roger said.

"So how did you put Kolev's bona fides in doubt?"

"We went to the interrogation center and told Kolev we had decided to give him a chance to redeem himself, and if he went on one more mission for us, we would still honor our initial agreement: five thousand dollars for the mission, three years in the Army and our support for citizenship. He jumped at the offer. He would have agreed to anything to get out of that cell and back to Bulgaria.

"Complicating his life was the fact that a Greek interrogator—I think his name was Mitsos, something, I forget now—was harassing the hell out of him. We heard he was driving Kolev nuts. Mitsos was a superb interrogator, but he was a creep, and he hated Bulgarians. He was tall and skinny, and always dressed in a black suit. He looked more like an undertaker than an interrogator. One of the guards told us that Mitsos would go to Kolev's cell in the middle of the night and turn on the light. When Kolev woke up, there would be Mitsos, staring at him. Mitsos would say something like, 'I'll be staring into your eyes when you drop through the trap door of the gallows.' Then he would turn off the light and leave. Some nights he would turn on the light and throw a rope into Kolev's cell with a hangman's noose at the end. So, we were anxious to get Kolev out of there.

"We took him out of the center and put him back in the safehouse. During the next week or so we briefed him on the mission. He was so eager, you would have thought we had just told him he had won a million dollars."

Roger said they had learned from many sources that when the Bulgarians caught anyone crossing the border, they took them to a lockup in Sofia. Some Bulgarian-speaking Greeks escaped from Greece to Bulgaria from time to time to avoid Greek criminal charges. At the lockup the Bulgarians always took their clothing away to be searched. They opened all their trouser, shirt and jacket cuffs. They even took heels off their shoes, looking for concealment devices.

"So when we issued Kolev the clothing for his mission, we concealed half of a U.S. five-dollar bill in the heel of his left shoe. In the cuff of his jacket we concealed four frames of exposed film, wrapped in aluminum foil.

"We knew the Bulgarians would find them, and Kolev couldn't explain how they got there. From the way Kolev had described his relationship with the colonel, we hoped the colonel would save him from severe punishment, even though the DS could never trust Kolev again. We wanted the colonel to realize that we were sending him a message: this operation is over."

"Is that the end of it?"

"The entire story, Jack."

"Do you think I should go out there and discuss this case with them?"

"Yes."

"Okay, Roger, then we must decide what we want to tell the Bulgarians about all this. We don't want to stonewall them. What do you think about this case now?"

"For God's sake—what do I think about this case now? The Cold War is over; the Communist regime is gone, the colonel must be retired or dead, and the old

DS has been dissolved. Let's say whatever we must to get the guy out of prison. Let's tell them the whole story."

"I don't know, Roger. If we tell them Kolev volunteered to work for us, that he was not coerced, they may not be too thrilled with him."

"Then tell them we coerced him. Tell them we threatened to kill him, if that's what it takes," Roger said, his eyes blinking.

"I'll just tell them we coerced him. But I presume I should tell them he broke and confessed when he came back from the mission."

"Yes, tell them that he confessed. Also tell them that's why we sent him back, to get rid of him, and the second mission was bogus, that we put the stuff in his clothing, and Kolev knew nothing about them. And find out if you can what happened to—what's, his name—Atanasov, and assure them that he was totally innocent. Even if he was a Communist activist then, he probably isn't one now."

"Okay. I'll arrange the trip. I'll probably leave early next week."

"Good, Jack. It's the right thing to do. Let me know as soon as you get back." The two men shook hands.

Epilogue

▼

Central Prison, Sofia, Bulgaria

The officer of the day called the orderly who was sitting outside his office. "Go get prisoner Kolev in cell 147, and take him to interrogation room five," he said. "There's someone there waiting to interview him. You wait outside the interrogation room and return the prisoner to his cell when they're finished."

The guard handcuffed Kolev and took him to the interrogation room. Behind the desk sat Stoyan Markov from the State Prisoner Review Board. He ordered the guard to remove the handcuffs and told Kolev to sit down. The guard departed.

When the guard closed the door both men stood and shook hands, smiling. Markov patted Kolev's shoulder and asked, "How've you been?"

"Good, good," Kolev answered, "and thanks for coming back."

Markov said, "It's been three months since we last talked, and I have news for you."

"Oh?" Kolev propped his elbows on the desk and rubbed his hands. "I hope it's good."

"It is. Now listen. Your case was carefully reviewed, and I've been instructed to advise you that it has been forwarded to a judiciary panel for consideration."

"What's that mean?"

"First, let me tell what it doesn't mean. No improprieties were discovered in the judicial process that led to you being sentenced to life in prison."

"Improprieties?"

"Yes, improprieties. It means nothing wrong was found regarding the trial. But new evidence has been presented that will lead to your conviction being overturned. This is highly unusual. In fact, I hear it is unprecedented."

"Are you serious? Really?" Kolev stood, knocking his chair over.

Markov nodded. "But please sit down. This won't take long."

Kolev recovered his chair and sat, his lower lip quivering. "What's the new evidence?" he asked.

"It is evidence confirming your statements that you were coerced by the Americans to undertake an illegal entry into Bulgaria for the purpose of engaging in espionage. It also declares you had no knowledge of the half of an American five-dollar bill and frames of exposed film discovered by the security service concealed in your clothing."

"They were in my clothing?"

"Yes. And the judiciary panel will determine that the court was correct to convict you of illegally escaping from Bulgaria, which at that time was a punishable offense, with a maximum prison term of three-to-five years. The panel will determine that you've already served the sentence, obviously, so you won't be retried. In fact, since you've been in prison new laws have been passed that allow any citizen to leave Bulgaria whenever he or she wishes, with a valid passport."

"What's it all mean?" Kolev asked. He clasped his hands to keep them from shaking.

"It means, Ivan, that you will be released from prison. You are to be a free man."

Kolev's eyes filled with tears. He lowered his head, and for long moments said nothing. He started to speak, but his voice cracked. He cleared his throat and said, "Mister Markov, I'll never be able to thank you enough; I never thought this moment would come. It'll take some time to really sink in."

"Ivan, you needn't thank me. I just managed the review of your case. I didn't discover this new information. It was presented to me."

"Really, who gave it to you?"

"Our intelligence service told us it came from the CIA. The CIA confirmed your story. They said you were coerced to undertake an espionage mission for them, and they concealed the currency and film in your clothing. They did it because you confessed to them that the old DS had recruited you, and sent you back to Greece as their agent. They had to get you out of Greece, they said, to avoid your execution by the Greek government, and to ensure that you never returned to Greece."

"The Americans said they coerced me to go on a mission for them?"

"Yep. They said you had no interest in working for them, and that they threatened to keep you locked up until you agreed."

"I can't believe this," Kolev took out a handkerchief and dabbed his eyes.

"Well it's all true. Congratulations, but I want to ask you this: At our initial meeting you lied to me when you said the Americans believed you when you reported to them after your first mission. I presume all you told me about their interrogation of you was a lie, correct?"

"I'm sorry. I did lie, except for how they interrogated me. It didn't take the Americans long to find out that I had not completed the mission by myself. Because they questioned me in such detail, I couldn't answer their questions. They knew I had not walked the entire route of my mission. The colonel had done his best to help me, but I could never have got by their interrogation unless I had actually walked the mission and made compass readings and notebook entries as I walked. It was impossible."

"Then, you didn't spend five months in the house by the sea with that man Petros, waiting for the Americans to give you another mission?"

"No, sir. I was locked in the interrogation center for five months, without anyone visiting me."

"What did this Petros say to you when it was discovered that you had been recruited by the colonel and sent back to Greece—or was he told?"

Kolev looked down at the table. "It was terrible," he said. "When the Americans were satisfied I had told them everything, they told me they were going to take me to the interrogation center. They told me to walk with them to the jeep, and didn't allow me to get my toothbrush, razor or anything. The Bulgarian was ahead of me and the American behind me. Petros was waiting on the veranda. They paused and said something briefly to Petros. Then Petros lunged at me, yelling, '*Kommunista! Kommunista!*' and he tried to grab me. His eyes were like fire, and I know he would have killed me if he could've. But the American and the Bulgarian held him and talked to him for a few moments, and when they released him he glared at me. It broke my heart. I couldn't look at him as they led me away. When they took me to the house the week before they sent me back, Petros wasn't there. One of the Greek drivers stayed with me."

"How did you intend to convince the colonel that you couldn't go back to Greece?" Markov asked. "If those items hadn't been found in your clothing, he planned to send you back to Greece to continue your work for him."

"I know. I was afraid to tell the colonel that I confessed to the Americans. It would've made me look like a traitor, so I was going to ask him not to send me back to Greece, to say it was very dangerous and I was afraid. He may not have respected me, but I didn't think he would force me to go back. But, as you know, there was no chance to say anything."

"Well, I don't know, Ivan, if you had pulled it off, you would've been trying to deceive both sides. It was a dangerous game. You probably would have ended up dead."

"I realize that now. I was pretty stupid." Kolev ran a hand through his hair and wiped another tear from an eye. "Mister Markov," he said, "before you leave, can you tell me what happened to the man I was to contact in Ruse? The man named Atanasov. Was he sent to prison also?"

"No. He was sentenced to death and shot," Markov said.

"Ooh, that's terrible. I'm sorry."

After a long pause the two men began to speak at once, and Kolev asked: "What, Mr. Markov?"

"I was only going to ask what you intend to do."

"I have no idea. I don't know where to start to look for a job, or even if anyone will hire me now that I've been in prison so long."

"Well, Ivan, I have one more thing to tell you. The Americans have arranged to offer you a job at the American Embassy as a local employee, a driver. The pay is remarkably good. When you're released you might want to go there to inquire, if you have any interest. Just ask for a man named…" Markov read from a scrap of paper: "Ask for a man named Robert Yost. You should be freed within the month."

Markov and Kolev stood, shook hands and embraced, patting each other on the back. As Markov started for the door he turned and said, "I've enjoyed my work very much this day."

Kolev couldn't speak.

Markov left, and the guard led Kolev to his cell.

THE END

0-595-65732-X

Printed in the United States
1357800001B/143